BACK TO THE FUTURE PART II

A NOVEL BY
CRAIG SHAW GARDNER
BASED ON A
SCREENPLAY BY
BOB GALE
STORY BY
**ROBERT ZEMECKIS
& BOB GALE**

BERKLEY BOOKS, NEW YORK

BACK TO THE FUTURE PART II

A Berkley Book/published by arrangement with
MCA Publishing Rights, a Division of MCA, Inc.

PRINTING HISTORY
Berkley edition/November 1989

ISBN: 0-425-11875-4

A BERKLEY BOOK® TM. 757,375
Berkley Books are published by The Berkley Publishing Group,
200 Madison Avenue, New York, New York 10016.
The name ''BERKLEY'' and the ''B'' logo
are trademarks belonging to Berkley Publishing Corporation.

PRINTED IN THE UNITED STATES OF AMERICA

10 9 8 7 6 5 4 3 2 1

The only thing more uncertain than the future is the past.

—SOVIET PROVERB

• PROLOGUE •

Great Scott!

Doc Emmett Brown never thought it would come to this.

It had all started so simply. Doc Brown still remembered the first night he had conducted the time experiment—all the way back in 1955.

A storm, which had been brewing all evening, was about to break.

The clock tower read 10:04.

The DeLorean, with its special super-conducting electrical pole added for the occasion, raced toward the electrical line.

And lightning struck the clock tower!

At the last possible second, Doc Brown connected the cables.

The hook on the pole above the DeLorean hit the

electrical line—and 1.21 jigowatts of electricity flooded into the flux capacitor . . .

And the DeLorean vanished into the future, leaving only twin trails of fire where its wheels had been!

Ah, that was a great day for science! Of course, Doc hadn't invented the DeLorean time machine in 1955. Heavens, DeLoreans didn't even exist in 1955! No, it was his 1985 counterpart—a Doc Brown thirty years older and wiser—who had finally perfected the flux capacitor, and found something powerful enough to fuel the device—plutonium! There had been a couple of unforeseen problems—experimental science was like that, after all—and Marty McFly, Doc's assistant in 1985, had ended up traveling back thirty years in time.

That's when all the complications began. But who knew they would come to this!

Oh, there had been problems back in 1955. When Marty had shown up, and his mother-to-be had developed a crush on her son-to-be, rather than on George McFly, as she was supposed to, it had threatened the existence of the whole McFly family. The situation had been very dramatically shown in a photo Marty had had of himself and the other two McFly children. As Marty got farther and farther away from the past as it should have been, the three kids faded more and more out of the picture, as if they had never existed!

Doc considered that little photo a perfect example of a paradox—doing something when traveling in the past to make the future, as we know it, impossible. Luckily, Marty and Doc had been able to correct that problem in the nick of time. Oh, if only that had been the only problem he'd found!

If only Doc hadn't been so curious, and gone into the future!

But he had, so there was no turning back. He had thought, for one brief instant, of ignoring the whole thing, pretending it had never existed. But Marty McFly was his friend—the boy had saved his life, for heaven's sake—and when something this devastating . . .

Doc shook his head. His decision had been made. Once he knew about some problem, he just had to attempt to correct it. After all, there was no other way for a responsible scientist to act!

He climbed into the DeLorean and set the destination display for 1985, on the morning following the time Marty returned. There was no reason, after all, for Marty not to get a good night's sleep.

They would be very careful, Doc told himself, and there would be no mistakes. While he had been in the future, Doc had done some research into the nature of time paradoxes, and discovered their results could be far more devastating than he had ever imagined!

But even Dr. Emmett L. Brown, with all of his intellect, could not envision the startling repercussions that would develop from what he was about to do.

• Chapter
One •

Everything—but *everything*—was different now!

The truck was the clincher. It was a new Toyota Four-By-Four, jet-black and gorgeous. And his parents had said that it belonged to him!

Marty McFly still couldn't believe how much had changed.

Before he had gone into the past, his father had been—Marty had to face it—a wimp who liked to spend his time laughing at Jackie Gleason reruns; a wimp who let his co-worker Biff run all over him. His dad had actually done the reports and office work for both men. And his mother had reacted to all this by quietly stepping back from life. She had also started drinking more than she should. They had both been good parents, had raised Marty and his brother and sister the best they could, but still . . .

Before he had gone into the past! How easily he accepted all that now. It had started with his friend Doc Brown—a local inventor whom everybody around Hill Valley thought was a bit of a crackpot, even for California. Anyway, Doc had wanted Marty to bring along his video camera to tape the doc's latest experiment: turning a DeLorean into a time machine! And, unlike most of Doc's other experiments, the machine had actually worked, sending Doc's sheep dog, Einstein, one minute into the future!

That's when the terrorists had shown up. It seemed that Doc had needed some plutonium for his time machine to work, so he had gotten these guys to steal some for him, vaguely promising he would make them some bombs or something. Doc had then planned to lose himself, so that the terrorists could never find him.

The terrorists, unfortunately, had had other ideas.

They had shot Doc—not fatally, as it turned out—and chased Marty after he had climbed into the DeLorean, forcing him to speed away from their machine guns and rocket launchers, until the car was flat out doing eighty-eight miles per hour. And, at eighty-eight miles per hour, the DeLorean had turned into a time machine, sending Marty thirty years into the past!

He'd come close to blowing it all in 1955, but had managed somehow to get through the whole thing okay, with a little help from the 1955 version of

Doc, who had also succeeded in sending Marty and the DeLorean back to the present, good old 1985.

Except that 1985 wasn't the same anymore. Now his father was no longer a wimp. Instead, he was a published science-fiction author. And his mother wasn't drinking anymore, and she looked much thinner and years younger! Heck, now his parents even played tennis together!

Biff had changed jobs, too. He now ran an auto detailing service, doing specialty work on cars. And Biff wasn't bullying anybody into doing his job anymore; in fact, he was sitting in the McFly kitchen at this very minute, having a cup of coffee before he started to wax George's car.

Even Marty's brother and sister had cleaned up their acts. And Marty's dream truck was sitting in the garage!

All this stuff had happened to his family and Biff, just because Marty had messed up a little bit when he had been stuck in 1955. They had been lucky that time, and everything had worked out all right. Marty knew that Doc Brown was right; it was dangerous to fool around with time.

But Doc was already gone again, off into the future. The future, not the past, had been the DeLorean's original destination, and Doc was eager to get on with his experiment. Still, Marty wished Doc had waited awhile, at least until everything had quieted down around here. The way all these things had changed—Marty thought they were great and all, but still—if you looked at it a certain way, all this change could be a little scary.

What if something else, something really serious, was wrong with this version of 1985? With all that had already happened, who knew what else could be different?

"How about a ride, mister?"

At the sound of the girl's voice, Marty turned away from the truck. It was Jennifer. Jennifer, with her long, auburn hair and big, brown eyes, looking every bit as pretty as the last time he had seen her. In Marty's humble opinion, she was the prettiest girl in all of the senior class.

It also didn't hurt one bit that she was Marty's girl friend.

Some things, then, were still the same—some very important things.

"Jennifer!" Marty had to keep himself from jumping up and down. "Oh, are you a sight for sore eyes! Let me look at you!"

Jennifer took a worried half-step away as he hurried over to her.

"Marty—" she said with a bit of a frown, "you're acting like you haven't seen me in a week!"

"I haven't!" Marty answered without thinking.

She looked at him even more strangely.

"Are you okay? Is everything all right?"

That's right! Marty realized there was no way she could know about everything that had happened to him. He had spent a whole week back in 1955, but he'd actually come back to 1985 at almost the same time he had left. So, to somebody who had stayed put in 1985, instead of jumping around in time like Marty and the DeLorean, it was like he hadn't been gone at all.

How did you explain something like that to someone without sounding absolutely crazy?

But everything was all right—in a way it had never been before, with his parents, with Biff, and the truck, too! He looked back at the house and smiled.

"Oh, yeah!" he answered her. "Everything is great."

It was especially great, with Jennifer, here and now. He hadn't realized until this moment how much he had missed her when he had been in the past. But he would make up for all that, and more, now that he was back where he belonged.

He put his arms around Jennifer. She put her arms around him. They looked into each other's eyes. Marty leaned his head forward toward Jennifer's slightly opened lips. He closed his eyes.

Jennifer would never believe how long he had waited for this kiss.

Their eyes opened abruptly as not one, not two, but three sonic booms rocked the driveway on which they stood.

Marty knew those sonic booms all too well. He looked around for the source of the noise, and saw Doc Brown pull the DeLorean into the driveway.

But both Doc and the DeLorean were different! For one thing, the car had a new addition to its rear deck, right above the engine, a white canister labeled "Mr. Fusion". And Doc (as white-haired and disheveled as ever—at least that was the same!) was dressed in even wilder clothes than he usually wore: a metallic yellow shirt covered by a long orange robe.

Doc jumped from the car.

"Marty!" he called frantically. "You've got to come back with me!"

Marty looked from Jennifer to Doc and back again. Back with Doc? In the time machine? He had thought this was all over!

"Where?" Marty asked.

"Back to the future!" Doc replied, as if going to the future were the most obvious thing in the world. The inventor didn't wait for Marty's answer, but walked quickly to the garbage can by the side of the driveway. He threw off the lid and began rifling through the can's contents.

"Wait a minute!" Marty called. "What are you doin', Doc?"

Doc picked up a banana skin and a crushed beer can. "I need fuel!" He carried the trash over to the "Mr. Fusion" canister, dumped in the banana skin and remaining beer, then—after a moment's thought—the beer can, too.

"Go ahead!" he shouted to Marty. "Quick, get in the car!"

Doc *really* wanted Marty to go to the future? But Marty couldn't! Not now, not after all he'd been through!

"No, no, no, Doc," Marty objected with a shake of his head. "I just got here. Jennifer's here!" He waved at the Toyota in the garage. "We're gonna take this new truck out for a spin."

Doc paused in his garbage collection for a moment to stare at both of them intently. "Well, bring her along! This concerns her, too!"

This concerned both of them?

Marty looked at Jennifer. She looked back at him.

"Wait a minute, Doc!" Marty interrupted. This might be more serious than he had thought. "What are you talking about? What happens to us in the future? Do we become assholes or something?"

Doc hesitated for a second: Should he tell them the truth? Then he blinked rapidly and shook his head. "No, no, you and Jennifer both turn out fine. It's your kids, Marty. Something's got to be done about your kids!"

Our kids?

Marty looked at Jennifer.

Jennifer looked at Marty.

Our kids?

They both got in the car.

Marty looked quickly at the inside of the DeLorean as he and Jennifer crowded into the passenger seat. It looked pretty much the same way it did before, with the three digital readouts on the dashboard showing where they were set to travel in time, along with where they were now, time-wise, and the last place—or rather, time—where the DeLorean had been. And the flux capacitor—the yshaped gizmo that made this time travel stuff possible—was still glowing behind them.

Doc jumped into the driver's seat, quickly setting the time circuits to send them into the future. He backed the car out of the driveway and started down the suburban street, heading straight for the dead end!

"Doc," Marty reminded him, "you'd better back up. We don't have enough road to get up to eighty-eight."

"Roads?" Doc replied with a laugh. "Where we're going, we don't need roads."

He reached out to the dashboard and flicked a switch that Marty didn't recognize. There was a sound outside the car. Marty leaned over the top of the door just enough to see that the wheels were rotating ninety degrees to flatten beneath the bottom of the car.

That meant the tires were no longer touching the ground.

That meant they had to be flying!

Doc gunned the car into the sky.

Marty and Jennifer looked at each other.

Nobody would ever believe this.

The DeLorean rose higher, with all three of them inside, too busy and excited to look where they had come from. Behind them, Biff Tannen walked out of the house, the new matchbook he'd just had printed, "Biff's Auto Detailing," held proudly in his hand. And not one of them, Doc, Marty, or Jennifer, turned back to see Biff, the matchbook forgotten in his hand, as he watched open-mouthed while the DeLorean soared upward into the sky, then disappeared into the future.

But even if they had noticed him, none of them could have seen Biff's eyes narrow as he wondered how a DeLorean could fly. None of them could have heard him mutter, "What in the hell is going on here?" And certainly none of them could have remotely imagined the dire consequences that were to arise out of Biff having witnessed their departure.

• Chapter
Two •

The first thing they saw were the lights. Big, bright lights, coming right for them, even though they were still flying.

There had been a triple flash of white light, followed by pouring rain. Marty realized they must be in the future. But all they could see was the rain, and those lights.

The glowing circles got larger still, and Marty could see they were attached to something even bigger, something that looked like nothing so much as a flying tractor-trailer. Whatever it was, it was bigger than big. And it was coming right toward them.

Both Marty and Jennifer screamed.

Doc jerked the wheel of the DeLorean to the right. The two vehicles missed each other by inches. The driver of the monster vehicle stuck his head out the window.

"Stay in your own lane, maxhole!"

Own lane? Marty leaned forward, trying to get a better view of the rain-swept sky. Yeah, there were floating lane markers out there, small orange cones simply floating in the air.

"What was that?" Marty asked as soon as he managed to breathe.

"Teamster," Doc replied.

"But we're flying!" Marty objected.

"Precisely!" Doc swung the DeLorean over to the correct side of the lane markers.

A new voice shouted angrily at them:

"DeLorean, vector twelve, this is air-traffic control!"

The voice was coming from the middle of the dashboard. Marty realized it must be some sort of radio.

"You've made unauthorized entry into commercial transport airspace," the angry voice went on. "Why the hell wasn't your transponder on? Over!"

Doc grinned at Marty and Jennifer before he replied.

"Roger. We're experiencing minor technical transponder difficulty. We're descending now for repair. Over and out!"

Marty admitted it; he was more than shaken up, and not just with that huge, flying truck. Commercial transport airspace? Transponder?

It was time for some answers.

"What the hell's going on, Doc?" Marty demanded. "Where are we? *When* are we?"

Doc pointed at the time display as he eased the nose of the DeLorean downward.

Marty read the digital display:

OCTOBER 21, 2015. 4:29 P.M.

"We're descending toward Hill Valley, California," Doc repeated much too calmly, "on Wednesday, October 21, 2015."

"2015?" Marty repeated. "You mean, we're actually in the future?"

They were suddenly surrounded by flying passenger cars that didn't look all that different from the DeLorean. They must be down in the noncommercial air lanes now. The cars seemed to be going much too fast in all this rain, but then, Marty realized, there weren't any roads to slip on anymore, were there?

An old, beat-up heap with a noisy muffler zipped past them, its dented rear end covered with bumper stickers:

I BRAKE FOR BIRDS!

LITTERING CAN KILL!

THIS SUMMER, DO SOMETHING A ROBOT CAN'T DO—
PICK GRAPES!

Littering could kill? Marty looked down from the window of the DeLorean. He guessed almost anything could kill if you dropped it from this height.

Marty had to face it. He was having a little trouble coming to grips with all this.

Sure, he had traveled through time before, but that

had been into the past, where he'd met younger versions of his parents and other people from Hill Valley. Everybody remembered the past. It was just something you accepted as being there. But traveling to the future—he was someplace where stuff hadn't even happened yet!

Jennifer turned from where she, too, had been gazing out the window. She looked at both Marty and Doc with that same, cautious expression Marty had seen when he announced he had been gone for a week and she had seen him the day before.

"The future?" she asked tentatively. "Marty, what do you mean? How can we be in the future?"

Marty tried to think of a good way to explain things. He decided there wasn't a good one.

"Oh, well," he tried anyway, "you see, this is actually a time machine." He patted the dashboard.

Jennifer continued to stare at Marty. "Doc built a time machine out of a DeLorean?"

Marty grinned and shrugged. "That's Doc."

"I figure if you're gonna build a time machine in a car," Doc agreed cheerfully, "why not do it with some style!"

"And this is the year—2015?" Jennifer pointed at the main digital time display.

"October 21, 2015," Doc repeated with a hint of pride at his accomplishment.

"So, like, you weren't kidding? We can actually find out what happens to ourselves!" Jennifer got this funny little smile.

"Now, did you say we were married? And we've got kids?"

Her smile got larger, as if she liked the idea.

"How many kids?"

She giggled.

"Was it a big wedding?"

She was getting really excited now, looking all around Hill Valley as the car descended.

"Where do we live? Are we happy?"

She turned back to Marty, her eyes almost too bright.

"What about—"

Doc leaned over, holding a silver, penlight-sized device in front of Jennifer's face. The penlight-thing strobed a blue light in Jennifer's eyes.

Jennifer slumped in her seat, sound asleep.

"Doc!" Marty objected. "What are you doing?"

"Relax, Marty," Doc Brown reassured him. "It's just a sleep-inducing alpha rhythm generator. She was asking too many questions. No one should know too much about their future." Doc glanced at her again. Jennifer snored softly. "This way, when she wakes up, she'll think it was all a dream."

All a dream? Marty still didn't understand.

"Jeez, Doc, then why bring her?"

"I had to do something!" Doc insisted. "She saw the time machine, and I couldn't just leave her with that information." He gave Marty his best mad-scientist grin. "Don't worry. She's not essential to my plan."

Marty looked doubtfully at the smiling doc and

the sleeping Jennifer. Still, he had to have some faith in his inventor friend. After all, this was the same man who got him safely out of the past and back to good old 1985—even though Marty hadn't stayed there.

"Well," Marty replied slowly, "you're the doc."

Doc Brown turned his attention to the controls as they began their final descent. They landed in an alley between two buildings, an alley that didn't look all that different from alleys in 1985.

Doc flipped off half a dozen switches.

"First," he told Marty, "you're gonna have to get out and change clothes."

"Doc!" Marty pointed at the ongoing flood on the other side of the windshield. "It's pouring rain!"

"Oh, right."

Doc glanced at his watch.

"Wait three more seconds."

The rain stopped. Doc's head bobbed with satisfaction.

"Right on the tick." He glanced wistfully up at the sky. "Too bad the post office isn't as efficient as the weather service."

Doc and Marty pushed open the DeLorean's gull-wing doors. Marty climbed out of the car. But when he turned back to Doc, it looked like the inventor was peeling off his face!

"Excuse the disguise, Marty," Doc explained mid-peel, "but I was afraid you wouldn't recognize me. I went to a rejuvenation clinic and got an all-natural overhaul. They took some wrinkles out, did a hair repair, changed the blood—added a good thirty or forty years to my life. They also replaced my spleen and colon." He pulled the last of the goop from his face and ran a hand through his tangled hair. The hair stayed tangled. "What do you think?"

Marty had trouble not staring at the new, improved Doc Brown. Doc didn't look that different, really—Doc never looked that different—but he did look better. Younger. Many of the wrinkles were gone, and there was more of a sparkle in his eyes.

"You look good, Doc," Marty answered slowly. "Real good." As he stared at his slightly dewrinkled friend, Marty's surroundings really began to sink in. So this actually was 2015.

"The future!" It didn't look all that different in the alley. Marty guessed that alleys were alleys. The trash cans were a little newer and nicer, maybe. Marty bet it would be really different, though, out on the street. He took a couple steps away from the car. "Whoa, I gotta check this out!"

"All in good time, Marty. We're on a tight schedule here." Doc pulled a small silver satchel—sort of a gym bag of the future—from the back of the DeLorean. "Here're your clothes."

Marty looked back at the inventor. "So, Doc, like what about my future? I make it big, right?" He paused a minute, trying to figure out what would be his most obvious future. "I'm—what—a rich rock star?"

Doc waved the question away with his free hand.

"Please, Marty, no one should know too much about their own destiny."

"Sure, Doc. Right." That's right, Marty thought. Doc Brown had mentioned this destiny business before; that was the whole reason Jennifer was snoozing in the car. "But am I rich?"

Doc sighed. "Damn. Maybe I shouldn't be doing this. Maybe I should just forget this whole thing and take you back home."

Home? No way did he want to go home! Marty decided he'd better apologize.

"Hey, I'm sorry, Doc. I'm just excited, that's all. Everybody wants to know about their future."

"That's what I'm afraid of." Doc sighed again. He held the gym-bag-of-the-future out to Marty.

After looking at the bag for a second, Marty pulled open the Velcro seal.

"All right," Doc instructed, "take off your shirt, put on the jacket, the shoes, and the cap."

Marty set the bag down on the rear end of the DeLorean. As Marty started to unbutton his shirt, Doc leaned into the car beneath the open gull-wing door. A moment later, Doc lifted the still-sleeping Jennifer out of the passenger seat, placing her gently in a broad doorway on the alley's side.

Marty paused in his unbuttoning.

"You mean we're just gonna leave her?"

"It's too risky to take her with me," Doc answered regretfully. "Don't worry. She'll be safe. She's out of sight, and it'll just be for a few minutes."

Doc reached in his pocket and pulled out a plastic card with a pair of eyeholes, and the words "pocket binoculars" printed beneath. It looked like some cheap, plastic toy, the kind of thing you'd find as a prize in a cereal box. The way Doc handled it, though, Marty suspected it was really a more compact, fully functional future model.

Doc ran to the far end of the alley and peered through his card.

Marty pulled off his white-striped shirt, leaving only the purple T-shirt he wore underneath. He pulled the jacket from the bag, but, as he pulled it on, was somewhat distressed to realize it was four sizes too big and baggy, with sleeves that hung down to his knees. How could Doc expect him to wear something like this?

Marty shook the sleeves. Was there some way to roll them up or something? His fingers brushed against a small patch near the right cuff—a patch that read "uni-size form fit."

The jacket instantly shrank to fit, sleeves stopping precisely at the wrist as the coat's sides tailored themselves to his rib cage. After a moment's shock, Marty decided that this was more like it!

So what else did he have to put on? Marty pulled out a pair of future sneakers from the bottom of the bag.

Doc apparently had seen what he was looking for. He tucked his binocular card in his pocket, he hurried back to the car.

Marty had slipped the shoes on his feet, but they

were still loose, a lot like the jacket a moment ago, and he could see no way to tie them. Except there was a pad—like the one on his jacket—on the right sneaker. After a moment's hesitation, he pressed it softly.

The sneakers zip-laced themselves shut.

"Power laces!" Marty cheered. "All right!"

Marty pulled the cap from the bag, and stuffed his everyday shirt and shoes in its place. The hat looked more or less like a baseball cap, except for whatever shining fabric it was made of—a fabric that seemed to change color every time the cap moved.

Doc stood by the car. He appeared to be waiting for Marty.

"Okay, Doc," Marty asked obligingly as he stuck the cap on his head. "So what's the deal?"

Doc glanced at his watch, then pointed down to the far end of the alley. "In exactly two minutes, you go around the corner, into the Cafe 80's."

"Cafe 80's?"

"It's one of those nostalgia places," Doc explained, "but not done very well. Go in and order a Pepsi." Doc rummaged in his pocket, then pulled out a crumpled bill. "Here's a fifty."

Marty accepted the paper money. It looked more or less like the money Marty was used to—although Marty was a lot more used to handling tens and twenties than fifties. Doc was being awfully generous here. A fifty-dollar bill for a Pepsi? Oh, well. He probably wanted to make sure Marty had some money leftover in case of emergencies. Marty stuffed the fifty into the pocket of his jacket.

"Then wait for a guy named Griff," Doc continued.

"Griff," Marty repeated.

"Right." Doc nodded, pleased that Marty was taking this all in. "Griff's going to ask you about tonight—are you in or out? Tell him you're out." Doc raised his voice, as if this part was even more important than what he had said already. "Whatever he says, whatever happens, say no, you're not interested."

Doc waved at the alleyway. "Then leave, come back here, and wait for me." Doc's voice started to rise again. "Don't talk to anybody, don't touch anything, don't do anything, don't interact with anyone. And try not to look at *anything!*"

Doc was really serious about this not-messing-with-your-future business. Still, there were some things that Marty didn't understand.

"I don't get it, Doc. I thought this had something to do with my kids."

"Precisely." Doc rummaged in the gym bag. "In those clothes, you're the spitting image of your future son—I know, I just checked on him with my binoculars." He paused, staring at Marty quizzically. "Hmmm," he murmured, then grinned with a snap of his fingers. "Pull out your pants pockets."

Marty did as Doc asked.

"Perfect!" Doc declared.

Marty's eyes rose doubtfully toward the cap above his forehead. "I still don't get it, Doc."

"Well—" Doc replied hesitantly, "I guess there's no point in keeping it a secret."

He reached into another one of his pockets and pulled out a newspaper. It was a *USA Today*, Hill Valley Edition!

"LOCAL YOUTH JAILED IN ATTEMPTED THEFT!" the main headline screamed, and below that, in smaller letters, "Youth Gang Denies Complicity."

But Marty's eyes were drawn to the color picture immediately beneath, a photo of a kid who looked exactly like Marty!

• Chapter Three •

Marty realized he was staring. He pulled his gaze away from the photo to look back at Doc.

"My son? He looks just like me!" He looked back down at the paper and tried to read the story, but that only made it worse. What could he do if his son was in jail? "This is terrible! But, Doc, if this is already in the newspaper—"

Doc pointed at the date in the corner: October 22, 2015.

"This is *tomorrow's* newspaper," he explained. "That's why we're here today—to prevent this event from ever happening!"

Marty looked up from the paper again. *Now* he understood why Doc needed him!

He whistled softly. "Whoa, Doc, this is heavy."

"I know," Doc agreed grimly. "And it gets worse.

As a result of this, your daughter goes into a state of severe depression and commits—"

"My daughter?" Marty asked. This was getting to be beyond heavy! "I have a daughter? What does she do?"

Doc's watch beeped loudly.

"Damn!" Doc snapped his head down to look at the dial. "I'm late!"

He grabbed the newspaper and ran down the alley. "Doc, wait!" Marty yelled, trying to keep that touch of panic he was starting to feel from growing any larger. "Where are you going?"

"To intercept the real Marty Junior," Doc called over his shoulder. "You're taking his place!"

He disappeared around the corner.

"Marty Junior?" Marty mused aloud. "I name him Marty Junior? With a name like that, how could he go wrong?" Hey! There was no reason to panic. The kid had Marty McFly's genes, after all, right?

"Well," Marty added to console himself. "At least he's not a wimp."

But his son was about to make a really bad decision, and it was up to Marty to take his place and save him! The original Marty took a deep breath and walked out of the alley.

Even if it was 2015, he knew exactly where he was.

Directly in front of him was Courthouse Square! It had changed some in thirty years, but it was still easy enough to recognize. After all, he had skateboarded around these streets a thousand times or more in 1985, and even managed to do the same once or twice during the week he had spent in the 1950s. He wondered for a second if kids still skateboarded in 2015.

The village green had been mostly replaced by a large duck pond and a fountain, although the square was still bordered by those same hedges. The courthouse building was still there, too, but it looked like it had been turned into some sort of mall, with a fancy, smoked green glass entryway that led to dozens of underground shops. The names of the stores below flashed on a 3-D electronic display, places with names like World O' Transponders and Hydrators Unlimited.

There were still stores on the other three sides of the square, too, although most of the names had changed since 1985. The adult bookstore had been replaced by a shop called Bottoms Up, "Specializing in Plastic Surgery since 1998!", with signs in the windows advertising face-lifts and a today-only special on breast-implants.

And the movie theater had changed, too. It was called the Holomax now, and the marquee announced they now featured:

FULL HOLOGRAPHIC SCREENS!
★ Now Playing ★
JAWS 14
DIRECTED BY MAX SPIELBERG
★ This time, it's really, *really* personal! ★
DELIGHTFULLY AIR-CONDITIONED!

There was still a gas station on the corner, too, only now it was on the second story, above a Seven-Eleven! A car landed on the upper deck, and a dozen robot arms appeared, pumping gas, checking the tires, washing the windows. Farther up the street, there was a tavern called the Fusion Bar and a Century 22 real-estate office. On the other side of the square, Marty could see a robotics shop ("Sales, Service, Rentals!"), and a video software store, with a sign in the window advertising "The Video Classic: *A Match Made in Space!*" Wow, Marty thought. They'd made a movie out of his dad's book, too?

Most of the traffic seemed to have relocated itself overhead. Cars, some of which looked old enough to come from 1985, or even before, briskly flew back and forth across the air lanes. Marty could have sworn one of those fliers was an Edsel. There was a flashing sign overhead, advising drivers of current "Skyway Conditions." And there were billboards both up there and down close to the ground, too, pointing out the advantages of "US Air to Vietnam," complete with a smiling couple with surfboards—or "Earl Shieb IV will hover-convert any car! Just $3999!" or even "Pepsi-Perfect—it's vitamin enriched!"

Actually, there was only one thing in all of Courthouse Square that hadn't changed at all—except maybe to look a little older. The courthouse clock was still there at the top of the converted courthouse building, and still stopped at 10:04, the time lightning struck it back in 1955, letting Marty get back where he belonged, to 1985, at least for a few hours.

Marty stepped out onto the street. Well, maybe there were a couple other things that hadn't changed so much. Those folks dancing up there looked like Hare Krishnas. And the sign on the store directly behind the dancing guys in the saffron robes read: E-Z CREDIT FINANCE COMPANY. And one whole corner of the street had been completely torn up by the electric company.

But where was the Cafe 80's?

There was an antique store on this side of the street, a place called Blast From the Past. The front window of the place was full of things Marty remembered from 1985 or before, all carefully labeled, stuff like a Betamax VCR, a Super-8 movie projector, a lava lamp, a MacIntosh computer, and a whole bunch of Perrier bottles. In fact, the only thing Marty didn't recognize in the window was a small, silver book with the bold, red title: *Grey's Sports Almanac 1950–2000*.

Marty looked up the street. He still had an important job to do. Just beyond the antique store, on the corner where the aerobics place used to stand back in 1985, was the Cafe 80's.

Marty walked quickly to the cafe. The door slid aside to let him enter. Doc Brown had called this "one of those nostalgia places." The walls were painted in pastel pinks and greens straight out of that new cop show—"Miami Vice". But a lot of stuff here Marty either didn't recognize at all, or it somehow looked wrong.

He supposed some of it could have come from after 1985. That was weirder still, when he thought about it. He was in a nostalgia place for stuff that hadn't even happened yet! Like what were all these weird yellow squares pinned to one wall, squares that said stuff like "Baby on Board" and "Dead Wife in Trunk"? Why would anybody want to use that sort of thing?

The front counter in the place looked a lot like fast-food places Marty was used to from 1985—but he guessed that was the idea—with a big wall display overhead, complete with pictures of the burgers and other stuff they served. Every seat in the place, though, had a small video screen in front of it, sort of like a Watchman, and all the screens were showing images from the 1980s—news clips, movies, rock videos. The sound system was pounding out a song about heaven being only one step away, or something, that Marty thought sounded vaguely familiar. At least there was some good guitar work in it.

There was still something strange about this place, though. A good part of it, Marty thought, had to be the counter help. They weren't human, for one thing, but some kind of robots with large video screens that switched between showing human faces and food items. Beneath each robot's screen was a tray to carry food, but—for some reason—all of the robots also sported a pair of red metallic wings to either side of their screens. Wings? Marty hoped they were just there for decoration.

But Marty had come in here to do more than stare. He was supposed to order something. He walked up to the front of the restaurant.

One of the red-winged robots smiled at him from the other side of the counter. The thing's video-screen face resembled nothing so much as a computer-generated Ronald Reagan.

"Welcome to the Cafe 80's," the television image announced, "where it's always morning in America, even in the afternoon."

Music swelled behind the computer face, as what looked like an all-too-familiar political announcement from the 1984 presidential campaign played itself out behind the Reagan image.

"Our special today—" the Reagan-thing continued, "is mesquite-grilled sushi, cajun-style, dipped in Thai cilantro sauce."

Marty frowned. He didn't know what everything in that concoction was, but it sounded terrible! You weren't supposed to grill sushi, anyway, were you? There was maybe such a thing as having a little bit too much of the 80s.

The video image flickered and shifted, turning into this old guy with a beard and turban. It was the Ayatollah Khomeini!

"No!" the Ayatollah screamed. "It is the Great Satan Special! I demand you have *tofu*!"

The image shifted as the voice turned to a gentle falsetto. "Hey—be cool." The image resolved itself to approximate Michael Jackson. "Don't be *bad*. We're all friends here." The head bobbed around on the screen as if the unseen body beneath might be moonwalking.

Marty decided he should close his mouth and do what the Doc told him he should.

"Uh—" he managed. "Could I have a—Pepsi?"

He held up the fifty.

"Cash?" the screen—now once again in Reagan's image—replied doubtfully. "Well, it's much easier to just use your thumb—"

"My thumb? Huh?" Marty looked stupidly at his hand. "Uh, no, look, I'll just pay cash."

"Well, there's a handling surcharge on cash, but—" The Reagan-thing hesitated, as if truly considering Marty's plight. "Well, okay, we'll take cash."

The video creature pointed toward a tray on the counter. Marty placed the fifty there. It was instantly sucked out of sight. There was a quick series of electronic beeps, and a small panel whirred aside, revealing a covered, see-through plastic cup with the words PEPSI-PERFECT.

"And your change," Reagan's image continued cheerfully, "rounded off to the nearest five dollars."

A crisp, new five-dollar bill shot out of another slot. Forty-five dollars for a Pepsi? This really *was* the future.

Marty picked up the money and the cup. The cup's lid seemed to be permanently stuck to the top. He had no idea how to open it.

"Hey, McFly!" a very familiar voice yelled from behind him.

A very familiar voice? In the future?

Marty turned around and looked at the man sitting behind the plate of half-eaten sushi, a baseball game blaring from the Walkman by his seat. The fellow who had spoken to him was maybe seventy, seventy-five years old, but Marty would recognize that smirk anywhere.

It was Biff Tannen!

• Chapter Four •

"Biff!"

Marty walked slowly toward the auto-detailer, who now sported a head of thinning white hair and a full set of wrinkles.

"Yeah," Biff replied with a smirk unchanged by the years. "I've seen you around. You're Marty McFly's kid, huh?"

"Huh?" Marty replied, still in a bit of shock from having run into his past. "What?"

"Marty Junior," Biff replied in a tone that assumed Marty was too stupid to figure it out for himself. "You look like him, too. Tough break, kid." Biff's smirk got even wider. "It must be rough being named after a complete butthead."

Tough break? Butthead?

"What's that supposed to mean?" Marty demanded.

Biff picked up the cane that rested beside his feet. Marty noticed that the cane's brass handle was sculpted into a clenched fist. Biff lifted the cane and knocked it briskly against Marty's forehead.

"Hello?" Biff asked rather more loudly than necessary. "Anybody home? Think, McFly, think! Your old man—Mr. Loser!"

"What?" Marty was completely confused. What was Biff talking about? His father was a success now—a published author and everything—or at least he had been in 1985! Had the future changed things again? "A loser?"

"That's right." Biff seemed to be really enjoying himself now. "A loser, with a capital 'L'."

But Marty refused to believe it. "That can't be!" he insisted. "I happen to know that George McFly is no longer a loser!"

Biff looked up at the ceiling, as if he couldn't believe Marty's stupidity. "No," he explained even more slowly than before. "*George* McFly's never been a loser. But I'm not talking about George McFly. I'm talking about his kid—*your* old man! Marty McFly. Senior!"

Biff shook his head. "He just took his life and flushed it completely down the toilet." Biff's smirk faded for an instant, as if even he couldn't believe how far Marty senior had fallen.

Marty senior? But *he* was Marty senior! And he had flushed his life away?

"I did?" Marty asked. "I mean, he did?"

Behind Biff, Marty noticed a beat-up old convertible lowering itself—actually lowering itself, without wheels—into a parking space outside the window. A minute ago, he would have been fascinated by that sort of thing. But that was before he'd learned his life had gone down the toilet!

Four people got out of the car, three guys and a girl, and one of them walked directly into the Cafe 80's. He was a big guy. Huge. He wore black pants and a wicked looking jacket over a black chain mail shirt. Each of his boots was adorned with a sharp, metallic rhinoceros horn. A cap full of sharp metal spikes was strapped to his head.

"Hey, Gramps!" the newcomer yelled at Biff as he crossed the restaurant. "I told you *two* coats of wax on the car, not just one."

"Hey," Biff answered just as belligerently. "I put the second coat on last week!"

"Yeah," the younger man smirked, "with your eyes closed." He jerked his thumb toward the door. "Come out here and scan it. It's a lo-res job."

Marty knew that smirk. In fact, he knew the newcomer's every move. He had seen all those moves before, when he had met the teenage Biff back in 1955!

It was just like Marty's son looking exactly like Marty. This new kid looked all too much like . . . he didn't want to think it. Still, Marty had to ask— even though part of him really, really didn't want to know.

"Uh, are you two related?"

Biff frowned back at Marty. He lifted his cane again, once more knocking the silver fist against Marty's head.

"Hello?" he yelled even louder than the last humiliating time. "Anybody home?" He waved his cane at the boy. "Whaddya' think, Griff just calls me Grandpa for his health?"

Oh, shit. Marty looked over at the teenage Biff look-alike.

"*He's* Griff?" he whispered. *The* Griff that he had to face up to, to save his son? Doc Brown hadn't warned him that the future would be *this* bad!

Griff elbowed Marty out of the way to glower down at Biff.

"Gramps," he muttered darkly as he pointed toward the door, "nuke the bab-sesh and get out here, 'orrita! What the hell am I paying you for?"

He turned and looked at Marty with a gaze that held no kindness, no humor, no mercy—only contempt that something as low as a McFly should sully the face of the earth.

"And McFly—" He pointed a pudgy finger at Marty's chest. "Don't go anywhere. You're next!"

Marty got the strangest sense that this had all happened before. He remembered how, back in 1955, Biff used to rap his father George's head with his knuckles as he yelled "Hello? Anybody home?" Just like Biff had rapped on Marty's head with his knuckleheaded cane! And Biff's attitude back in 1955 was almost exactly like his grandson's, here in the future. Apparently, when you were a teenager in Hill Valley, you either did what a Tannen said, or you paid. Marty might be standing here in 2015, but it was just like the past, all over again!

Biff waved in Marty's direction as the two of them walked toward the exit.

"Listen Griff," the old man muttered, "don't you go loanin' that McFly kid any money—even though he probably needs it, him and his old man both."

Biff smirked back at Marty as his grandson led the way out the door.

"Hey kid! Say hello to your grandma for me!"

The door shooshed closed behind them.

Marty half-watched through the window, as Griff carefully pointed out all the spots on his car that Biff had missed. Griff's three sidekicks—a tall, oriental fellow with a shaved head; a girl with long blond hair, spiked bangs, and three-inch fingernails; and a shorter guy with a tattooed face who seemed to be wearing computer equipment as part of his clothes—all hung around in the background. Marty realized that was another similarity between the two generations. Teenaged Tannens always seemed to have a gang. And Tannens and their gangs always bullied McFlys.

But it didn't have to happen that way. Marty had changed things, unbalanced the equation, when he had ended up back in 1955. And he had to change things again, now that he was in the future. But how could he, if his future self had gone down the toilet? That strange sense of time-traveling déjà vu was back again, as if being trampled by a Tannen was his destiny, and maybe the destiny of every other McFly that had ever lived.

No. He had to shake himself out of that feeling. Doc had sent for him because he had beaten Biff Tannen in 1955, and he could beat Biff's grandson now. All he had to do was take it easy and follow Doc's instructions—and hope there was nothing else here in 2015 that would trip him up. Marty just wished he knew more about how the future really worked.

A rock video came on most of the tiny TVs around him. He recognized the group, Huey Lewis and the News, doing a song called "The Power of Love." It was a pretty good song, too. Marty nodded to the beat. He wouldn't mind just sitting here for a minute, listening to the music and drinking his Pepsi— if he could figure out some way to get the lid off the container.

Well, the music by itself would have to do. At least you could still count on some things.

Three girls in their young teens watched the video along with Marty. They didn't seem to share his enthusiasm.

"Oh, shred that!" one of the girls commented with a yawn. "I only scan that kind of vid at my grandma's!"

"Yeah," the girl next to her added, sounding even more bored by the whole thing than the first. "What do they call it? Rock and rail?"

The third girl shook her head in disbelief. "It doesn't even sound like music!"

"Yeah!" the first girl agreed. "Thank God we didn't have to live in the eighties." She rolled her eyes at the video. "It must have been terrible!"

Shred that? Terrible? Rock and rail?

Marty wondered what they listened to now, but he was afraid he didn't want to know. He suddenly felt very old and out-of-place. He looked away from the video screens and the girls who were too bored to bother.

Hey! Now this was more like it. Over in the corner was an old arcade video game called Wild Gunman, which Marty used to play in the Seven-Eleven in 1985.

A kid of eight or nine stood in front of the game, looking thoroughly confused. The kid glanced up as Marty walked toward him.

"How do you play this thing?" the boy asked.

Marty grinned. Now *this* was something he knew about! "I'll show you, kid. I'm a crack shot at this one." He stepped in front of the machine as the kid moved out of the way. But there was something different about this version of Wild Gunman. For one thing, Marty couldn't find the coin slot.

"Where do you put in the quarter?" he asked.

"Quarter?" the kid replied. "What's a quarter?"

Marty had no idea what kind of change they used in 2015. He moved his hand along the side of the game's console, feeling for something that would take the money. Didn't the coin slot used to be over here?

The game beeped to life as his thumb hit a metal plate. Oh—so that's what the Reagan robot meant by "use your thumb." The name WILD GUNMAN appeared on the screen, followed by the usual instructions and previous high score. Well, Marty would have to worry about financial questions later. Right now, he had a game to play!

He got into it right away, shooting every outlaw and gunfighter that showed up in the Western town on the screen. He'd give this kid from the future a real demonstration of video talent!

"You mean you have to use your hands?" the kid whined. "That's like a baby toy!"

Use your hands? Baby toy?

The kid wandered away.

Marty's hands fell from the controls. He suddenly felt older than old.

He supposed he might as well finish the game. Somehow, it wasn't the same. His eyes wandered from the video display. He saw himself walking on the other side of the window, right by Biff and Griff's gang, who were all too busy arguing to notice him. He headed straight for the door of the Cafe 80's.

Himself? On the other side of the window? Straight for the door? Marty realized he was looking at his future son—Marty Junior!

"Damn!" Marty whispered. He couldn't possibly let his future son see him; that could ruin all of

Doc's plans. But his son was coming in the only door that Marty saw in this place.

Where could Marty go?

He jumped behind the counter, dodging the Reagan automaton. He ducked down as his future son walked into the restaurant.

"Welcome to Cafe 80's" the Reagan-thing began, "where it's always—"

"Pepsi-Perfect," Marty Junior interrupted before the Reagan image could go into the whole routine.

"Hey, McFly!"

Marty Senior peeked above the counter long enough to see Griff and his gang walk through the door.

"Hi, Griff—" Junior replied hesitantly. "Guys. How's it going?"

Griff walked right up to him. "Hey, McFly, your shoe's unvelked."

Junior looked down at his sneakers as Griff flicked the other boy's nose with his index finger. The gang laughed. Marty couldn't believe it; his son fell for a joke that had been old back in 1955, when Biff used it on George McFly, Junior's grandfather! And it was worse than that. Even though he was the butt of the joke, Junior had laughed, too, along with the rest of them.

The déjà vu feeling was back, but this time it lurched around in Marty's stomach. There was something about Junior, something that reminded Marty Senior an awful lot of the teenaged George McFly, back in 1955. Maybe it was the way Junior's coat didn't quite seem to fit, like the coat's uni-size-form-fit patch was broken or something; or maybe it was those food stains on his white T-shirt; or the way his hair had been shoved, uncombed, under the color-changing cap. Yep, Marty Senior had to admit it. No wonder Griff picked on him. His son was a prime McFly nerd.

"So, McFly," Griff smirked, "have you made your decision about—tonight's little opportunity?"

Oh, no! This was what Doc had sent Marty to stop, and here he was hiding behind the counter while his son was out there with Griff, about to ruin his life!

"Uh, well," Junior began in the awkward voice he always seemed to use around Griff, "I'm still not sure. It seems kinda' dangerous—"

All right! Marty Senior thought. Way to go, son of mine! You tell them! Marty Senior almost cheered. Maybe Doc had been worried about this whole thing for nothing. No matter what he looked like, a son of Marty's had to have spunk!

"What's wrong?" The female gang member stared at Junior with a twisted grin. "You got no scroat?"

Griff nodded in a way that said yeah, anybody named McFly had to be scroatless.

"What's it gonna be, McFly?" he demanded. "You in or out?"

"Well—" Junior hesitated, his eyes darting from one gang member to another. "I don't really think I should, but I guess I should discuss it with my fath—"

That's right! Marty made a fist where he hid behind the counter. Marty Senior would tell his son just what to do, and he'd tell the gang where to go, too!

"Are you saying no, McFly?" Griff cut off Junior's ramblings.

"Uh," Junior muttered, "well, yes." He tried to smile politely. "That is, I'm saying, 'no, thank you.'"

Griff grabbed Junior's shoulders.

"Wrong answer, McFly."

He picked Junior up and tossed him over the counter! Junior crumpled with a groan a yard away from Marty.

Griff's gang laughed.

"Now, now," the Reagan video chided, "let's behave ourselves!"

Marty looked back at his future son. Junior lay there, eyes closed.

"Yeah, Griff," he muttered, "sure, whatever you say—"

No, no, Junior couldn't mean what he was saying. He was delirious!

And he was in no shape to face Griff again.

"Stay down and shut up!" Marty whispered in Junior's ear. His future son moaned softly with his eyes still shut.

It was up to Marty—Marty Senior, now. He took a deep breath and stood up.

Griff grabbed his jacket and pulled Marty back over the counter.

"Now," Griff began in a tone that suggested what little patience he had had was long since used up, "let's hear the *right* answer, or you're gonna get—" his free hand made a fist—"a knuckle brioche!"

Marty landed on his feet and shoved Griff back. Marty's hands automatically closed into fists, as well.

Griff and the gang all took a step back.

"Well, well, well," Griff murmured as his smirk returned. "Since when did you become—" he paused to glance knowingly at his gang members—"the physical type?"

Marty looked down at his clenched fist. He had to watch it. He wasn't acting like his son Junior would act. Doc Brown was right; this changing the future business was tricky. If Griff and the others got suspicious, it might spoil everything.

He opened his hand and raised it in a gesture of peace. But his voice was still firm as he spoke.

"Look, Griff, the answer's no."

"No?" Griff asked, the single syllable somehow slow and menacing.

"N-O," Marty spelled it out.

He turned and walked for the door.

"What's wrong, McFly?" Griff called after him. "Chicken?"

Marty stopped three feet short of the door. It had gotten awfully hot in here all of a sudden. He could feel his two hands wanting to make fists all over again, and this time, he knew those fists were serious!

Nobody, but nobody, called Marty McFly chicken.

"I told you he's got no scroat!" the girl crowed.

The other guy, the one wearing the computers, grabbed Marty's cap and pulled it off. He waved his prize for the others to admire.

Marty turned around to look at the gang. He had to control himself.

Griff's smirk bloomed into an evil smile.

"Chicken, McFly!"

Griff and his cohorts made clucking noises.

That was it. Future or no future, Marty didn't take that from anybody!

"Nobody calls me chicken!"

He rushed Griff.

The bigger kid grabbed something from his belt with his right hand and put it behind his back. Whatever it was, it didn't look very big. Still, Marty told himself to be careful.

Griff swung his right hand forward—only now it held a baseball bat! Marty had no time to wonder where the bat had come from. He barely had time to duck. Marty's foot snaked out, catching the bigger guy around the ankle. Griff's foot went out from under him. That, and the still-swinging bat, were his undoing.

Griff yelled and plummeted to the floor.

The rest of the gang stood, all in a line, and stared at Marty in shock.

Griff grunted as he got back to his feet. His face was flushed, a reddish purple mask of hatred. Somehow, he looked even taller than he had before.

"All right, punk," he said through his teeth, "you've been looking for—"

Uh-oh. Marty knew this was the end, unless he could come up with something—anything. But what?

He thought about his fights with Biff, and things that had worked back in 1955.

Back in 1955?

Marty was desperate.

"Hey, look!" he shouted, pointing past the Reagans.

Amazingly enough, this time Griff fell for it—just like his grandfather had so many years ago. He jerked his head in the direction Marty pointed.

Marty threw a punch. Griff twisted his shoulder into it, blocking Marty's fist with his arm. So, Griff hadn't fallen for it, after all—or not as much as Marty had hoped he would.

Griff reached for Marty with two hands that were much too large. Marty realized it was time for emergency tactics.

He kneed Griff in the groin.

Griff groaned deep in his throat as he fell to his knees.

Marty jumped around the fallen leader, shoving against the future hacker as he pushed his way through.

The rest of Griff's gang fell like dominoes. Marty ran from the restaurant, narrowly avoiding Biff as the oldster leaned into his wax job.

In a second or two, Marty knew, Griff and the

boys would be after him. He ran across the street, straight for the hedge that bordered Courthouse Square. Maybe he could hide behind it. He had to do something!

There were two young girls on the other side of the hedge. Both of them were drinking from straws attached to clear plastic cups. Marty was tempted for an instant to ask them how they got the darned things open.

Then he saw that each girl stood on her own streamlined skateboard-scooter, sort of a skateboard with a long handle attached to the front. Both skateboards were painted electric pink, and were a bit better aerodynamically designed than things he was used to in the past, but—really—they were not all that different from the scooter he had borrowed from a kid back in 1955.

And he could borrow one of these again. Griff and the others wouldn't have a chance. Once Marty got himself on a skateboard, nobody could catch him!

Marty jumped the hedge. He reached out for one of the scooters.

"Hey, kid, I need your—"

He stopped short when he realized the scooter had no wheels.

The girl took a step back as Marty picked up the scooter—or whatever it was. The handle was detachable. Marty took it off. He brought the plastic skateboard shape closer. It had a loop strap to put your foot in, and a brand name in large red letters:

MATTEL HOVERBOARD!

"Hoverboard?" he wondered aloud.

He dropped the hoverboard to the ground. It hummed softly, hovering a few inches above the grass.

"All right!" Marty shouted. This was a skateboard and more. Hey! So there were some worthwhile things in the future, after all!

He slipped his foot into the strap and kicked it up to speed. Yep, it was just like a skateboard, only—with no friction to slow down the wheels—it was faster! He headed toward the courthouse. Let's see Griff and the others catch him now!

"There he is!" he heard Griff yell from the doorway of the Cafe 80's. "Hey McFly! You're a dead file!"

Marty glanced back at them. Griff shook his baseball bat. Marty smiled at them and skated away. Griff and his three sidekicks ran after him.

Marty needed to gain a little more distance. He grabbed onto the bumper of a passing hovercar, swooping past Griff's three sidekicks, who couldn't stop and turn in time. But where was Griff?

The car turned the corner. There was Griff, waiting for Marty with his baseball bat!

Marty saw the swing coming. He let go of the car, swerving away from the flailing bat, straight toward an oncoming car!

There was no time to get out of the way. The car braked, the driver blasting his horn.

And the hoverboard rose over the fender and hood of the car, climbing the windshield and roof, then flying off the other side, straight for the park and duckpond in front of the courthouse!

Openmouthed—and a touch disoriented by what the hoverboard could do—Marty noticed Griff and his gang run to the gang leader's old car, and pull out three hoverboards of their own—big, ugly things with all sorts of attachments, all probably five times faster than the toy Marty was riding!

Maybe, Marty thought, he could lose them in the shops underneath the courthouse. He glided over the duck pond. The board slowed, then stopped. Marty looked down. He had run out of gas dead center over the water.

The computer guy laughed.

"McFly, you bojo," he yelled. "Those boards don't work on water—unless you've got the power!"

As if to demonstrate the meaning of power, Griff tossed his hoverboard to the ground. And what a hoverboard! It was three times the size of the board Marty was riding, with twin jets in the back, and fins beside, not to mention those spikes all around the edges. In fact, it didn't look much like a skateboard—or hoverboard—at all. It looked, Marty thought, a lot more like a chain saw. Trapped over the pond, he had plenty of time to read the name of the board, too, written in gold letters on a jet-black background: THE PIT BULL.

The board came to life with an electric growl. Griff climbed on, bat once again in his hand. He kicked off, running the board in a tight circle, then throwing the front tip of the Pit Bull into the air, doing the closest Marty imagined he could to a wheelie with a board that had no wheels.

Griff grinned at Marty. Marty tried to urge his own board to move some way, any way, but only succeeded in almost losing his balance. The board was stuck, and Marty was dead meat.

Griff grinned at the three members of his gang.

"Hook on," he said.

The two guys and the girl pulled three tow lines from the back of Griff's board as they climbed onto hoverboards of their own. Griff cocked his bat back.

"I'm gonna take his head off."

Griff gunned his board. The four of them came straight for Marty.

Marty was still stuck above the pond on a board that wouldn't budge! His eyes froze on Griff's bat, growing larger and larger with every passing second.

Marty, the soon-to-be-headless sitting duck.

•Chapter
Five•

Griff went into his backswing.

Marty balanced on the hoverboard, six inches above the duck pond. He was trapped.

Griff started his swing, ready to drive Marty's head out of the park.

There was only one thing Marty could do. He pulled his foot out of the hoverboard strap, and stepped completely off the board.

He dropped quickly into the pond. Water that was much too cold splashed around him as he fell. Griff's board buzzed above him, missing Marty's head by inches. And Griff couldn't stop his swing. His hoverboard lurched wildly, sending Griff and his hangers-on straight for the courthouse.

Marty closed his eyes as his head went under. He

had taken a breath on his way down—but how long could he stay under?

He opened his eyes underwater. The pond was very clear and clean. He couldn't see any sign of Griff or the others overhead—only clear blue sky.

In fact, it was very quiet out there.

He decided he'd better come up for air.

He opened his eyes again when he got above the water. There were three unoccupied hoverboards hovering near the pond.

There were also four brand new holes in the smoked green glass that covered the lower part of the courthouse shopping mall—one each, Marty guessed, for Griff and his three gang members.

And, to top it all off, there were a whole bunch of uniformed security guards running around in the wreckage. Even from his pond-level vantage point, Marty could tell that the guards were very unhappy.

Grabbing the pink hoverboard, which had remained hovering just above the water, Marty swam for shore. From the far side of the park, Marty could hear old Biff yelling, "Buttheads!" Marty wondered which particular buttheads Biff was referring to. Probably all of them.

Marty climbed out of the pond. He was drenched. His future clothing seemed to weigh four times as much as it did when he was dry. He dragged his soaking wet body over to the little girl who owned the hoverboard, who, along with her friend, seemed content to stand around and watch all the excitement. Marty pushed his damp hair out of his face as he held the board out to her.

"Thanks a lot, kid."

"Keep it!" she said as she held up her new possession, so large that she could barely lift it. "I've got a Pit Bull now!"

She and her friend both climbed on the monster hoverboard that had once been owned by Griff and zoomed away.

So now Marty had a hoverboard? He doubted Doc would let him keep it. Still, Marty tucked the pink board under his slippery arm; you never knew when this sort of thing would come in handy.

In the meantime, he might be a little wet, but his mission had been a success. He had told Griff and the others just where to go. Now all he had to do was meet Doc, and this future trip was history!

But there was something wrong with his jacket. It ballooned with air, as Marty heard twin fans whirring on either side of his rib cage. Hot air blasted up from the collar to his face and hair. A small, bright orange patch had lit on the cuff of his sleeve. The patch read: "Drying Mode."

Five seconds later, he was no longer wet. Hey! As far as Marty was concerned, this future stuff was getting better and better!

But it wasn't perfect here—not with what still bothered him. He knew that by saying "no" to Griff, he had managed to save his son. But he had also learned, thanks to Biff Tannen, that his own life had gone "down the toilet!" His son was safe, but what about him? Marty needed to do something about his own future!

"Save the clock tower!" an old man in mechanic's coveralls yelled as he walked back and forth in front of the courthouse. "Save the clock tower!"

What? They wanted to tear down the clock tower again? Marty figured that when the rest of the building had been turned into a shopping mall, that old, stopped clock had to have real historical value.

"Hey, kid," the old guy called as Marty walked past. "Can you thumb a hundred bucks to help save the clock tower?" He held out a silver box with the inscription, "Portable Thumb Unit."

Marty hesitated.

"It's an important piece of history," the other guy added earnestly. The circular name patch over his pocket said his name was Terry.

Marty remembered Doc's warning not to get involved in anything else in the future.

"No, sorry," he replied as he took a step away.

But Terry wasn't going to give up that easily.

"Kid," he asked, glancing back at the weathered tower, "you know the story? It was sixty years ago, November 12, 1955. Back then, a hundred bucks was worth something. I remember it because that old buzzard over there—"

He pointed across the street at Biff, who had started to polish Griff's car again.

"—tried to shaft me out of three-hundred bucks for fixing his car," Terry continued. "I *never* forget about money. Anyway, there was this big storm—"

"Yeah," Marty interrupted, "I know all about it. Lightning struck the clock tower at exactly 10:04."

"Hey," Terry replied a bit testily. "Don't tell me, kid. I was *there*."

"So was I," Marty added under his breath. He turned again to go—and stopped.

There, on the opposite side of the street, was a big screen showing baseball footage. Marty had seen that kind of special screen in ball parks; they were the latest thing back in 1985. He imagined that, here in the future, those big screens must be everywhere.

The baseball footage disappeared, replaced by a banner headline:

CUBS SWEEP MIAMI IN WORLD SERIES!

Huh? Things really had changed.

"The Cubs win the World Series?" Marty wondered aloud. "Against *Miami*?"

"Yeah." Terry nodded in a particularly wistful way. "A hundred to one shot. Who woulda' thought?" He shook his head regretfully. "Sure wish I could go back in time and lay some bets on them Cubbies."

Actually, Marty hadn't been thinking about the Cubs.

"No," he began, "I just meant that *Miami*—" He stopped himself, and stared at the other man.

"What did you just say?" Marty asked.

"I said," the man obligingly repeated, "I sure wish I could go back in time and put money on the Cubs."

Go back in time? Money on the Cubs?

"Yeah!" Marty agreed enthusiastically. He looked over at the Blast from the Past antique store. There, still in the window, was the digest-sized answer to all his future problems. He walked closer to get a better look, reading the dark red lettering on that silver cover even more carefully than before:

GREY'S SPORTS ALMANAC:
50 Years of Sports Statistics
1950–2000
Includes
Baseball, Football, Horse Racing, Boxing!

It was foolproof, thought Marty, the perfect moneymaking plan. He would take that book back to 1985 and have the results of every major sporting event until the end of the century. And next to the book was a sign in the window: "We buy antique bills and coins." So he could even pay for it from his own wallet. It was perfect! He'd make sure that his future didn't end up in the toilet.

Marty entered the antique store and told the saleswoman what he wanted.

She pulled the Sports Almanac out of the window display for Marty, and launched into a salespitch. "This one has a very interesting feature—a dust jacket." She pulled the jacket loose to show him. The actual cover underneath was identical in design to the dust jacket: silver, with red lettering and pictures of sports figures. "Books used to have these to protect the covers—of course, that was before they changed to dust-repellent paper," she explained, reattaching it. "And if you're interested in dust, we also have this quaint device from the 1980s: it was called a Dustbuster."

Marty eagerly took the Almanac from her. "No thanks, I'm just interested in sports," he said.

"A history buff, eh?" she asked.

"Something like that," Marty replied.

The lady gave him the book in a silver bag. The whole transaction only took a couple of minutes. He looked back at old Biff, still polishing Griff's car, as he headed out of the store, toward the alley and his meeting with Doc.

"A loser, am I?" Marty asked, half to himself. He opened the bag and took a quick look at the book that was his future guarantee. From now on, he would stay as far away from that toilet as possible!

Marty Junior stepped out of the Cafe 80's, still rubbing the spot on the back of his head where he'd hit the floor. He wasn't sure quite what had happened in there. One minute, he had just said no, and the next Griff had tossed him behind the counter.

After that, he had to admit, he had been ready to say yes to almost anything, but Griff and the other guys hadn't come back to get him! Instead, he vaguely remembered a whole bunch of shouting, and then, he guessed, everybody left. Well, whatever happened, it was lucky for Marty McFly Junior. Maybe, he thought, you really could say no to Griff.

Junior decided he wouldn't be so cowed by the bully the next time he ran into him.

Old man Biff looked up from where he was waxing his grandson's car to stare at Junior.

"What the hell?" Biff muttered. "Two of them?"

Two of them? Junior thought. What the hell did that mean? Two of what? Two Marty McFly Juniors? Was the old man seeing double or something? Or was he just crazy?

Junior laughed as he walked away. He bet the whole Tannen family was crazy.

Marty turned the corner into the alley and stopped.

Jennifer was still there, asleep, where Doc had left her. But she was no longer alone. Two women cops were getting out of their police car. They strolled over to where Jennifer was curled up, snoring peacefully.

"Tranked out, I'd say," one of the cops ventured. "Smell her ears."

The other cop obliged with a frown, but shook her head. "Nothing."

"Run a thumb check," the first one ordered.

The second cop lifted Jennifer's arm, then pressed the sleeping girl's thumb against the side of a small silver box.

A flat, machine voice spoke from the box, clearly but rapidly:

"Name: McFly, Jennifer Jane Parker. Address: 3793 Oakhurst Street, Hilldale. Date of birth: October 29, 1968. Arrests: none. Warrants: none. Convictions: none."

The second cop frowned up at her partner.

"Hey, did it just say her birthday was 1968? She's got one hell of a job! Wonder who her doctor is. My mother-in-law could use a lift like *this*."

The other cop laughed. "She couldn't afford work like that! That's a whole face and body job." She looked back at the still-sleeping Jennifer. "Well, she's clean. That means we take her home."

The cops picked Jennifer up and carried her to the police car.

"Oh, no!" Marty whispered as the police car took off—straight up. The cops had Jennifer, and were taking her home. Home? Who knew where home was?

He had to find Doc Brown right away!

He ran out of the alley, back toward the park.

"Marty!" Doc's voice called to him. "Over here!"

Marty spotted Doc over by the Cafe 80's. Doc had changed his clothes, and was wearing the sort of outfit, lab coat, Hawaiian shirt and all, that he used to sport back in 1985!

"Doc!" Marty called breathlessly as he ran to meet him. "We're in some serious shit!"

"What do you mean?" Doc pointed into the window of the cafe. "Did something go wrong in there?"

"In there?" Marty nodded. "Yeah! For one thing, the *real* Marty Junior showed up!"

Doc's eyes grew wide when he realized his mistake. "Great Scott!" He snapped his fingers in frustration. "The sleep inducer! Because I used it on Jennifer, there wasn't enough power left to knock your son out for the full twenty minutes. Damn!"

Doc shrugged and shook his head. "It's all my fault, Marty. I just assumed if we could get your son to say no to those guys, we could prevent the event that puts him in jail from ever happening."

"Doc, he *did* say no!" Marty insisted. "And just as he was gonna change his mind, that's when I got into it."

Doc raised his eyebrows. "Well, in *that* case—" He pulled the *USA Today* back out of his pocket, unfolding it to read the headline.

"Marty, look!" He hit the paper with the back of his hand. "It's changed!"

Marty looked over Doc's shoulder. The headline was different. It no longer said: "LOCAL YOUTH JAILED IN ATTEMPTED THEFT!" It now read: "LOCAL YOUTHS JAILED FOR RECKLESS HOVERBOARDING!" And the photo of Marty was gone, too, replaced instead by pictures of Griff and his gang—and a shot of the damage they had done to the courthouse. The photo of Marty Junior was gone!

Doc pulled out his binocular card to get a better look at the courthouse, and what looked to Marty like a robot, with a *USA Today* logo on its back, taking a picture of the wreckage. Marty realized that very photo must be the one that appeared in the new version of tomorrow's newspaper—the version they had right in front of them. But that was *weird*. How could something change when it hadn't happened yet? Marty decided he still didn't understand this time travel business at all!

Doc tucked the binocular card back in his pocket and grinned broadly.

"Proof beyond positive that we've succeeded!" he cheered. "Because this hoverboard incident has now occurred, Griff now goes to jail. Therefore, your son won't go with him tonight, and that robbery will never take place! Thus, due to the ripple effect, the newspaper is now altered!"

"The ripple effect?" Marty asked.

Doc nodded. "Just as the past affects the future, the future reverberates into the past."

Whoa. This was heavy. But Marty remembered something like this happening once before, when he had first messed things up in 1955.

"Kind of like that picture of me and Dave and Linda," he asked, "where my brother and sister started to disappear?"

"Precisely!" Doc patted his young cohort enthusiastically on the shoulder. "Marty, we've succeeded! Not exactly as I'd planned, but no matter. Mission accomplished!" He took a step toward the alley. "Let's get Jennifer and go home."

Oh, no! *That's* what Marty had meant to tell him!

"But that's just it, Doc!" Marty exclaimed. "The police took her away!"

Doc looked like Marty had just told him that one of his dogs had died.

"Great Scott! Are you sure?"

Marty glanced back toward the alley. "About a minute before I found you."

"Damn!" Doc snapped his fingers in frustration. "Those cops were the reason I didn't land the De-Lorean here." His voice dropped lower as he confessed, "Some of the modifications I've made on it aren't exactly street legal."

He waved for Marty to follow him into the alley. Once they were both out of sight of the courthouse, Doc pushed back his sleeve to reveal what Marty had thought was a wristwatch, but apparently also served as a remote control for the DeLorean. Doc twisted something on the wrist device, and the car appeared overhead, emerging from wherever Doc had hidden it behind the buildings. Doc pressed something else on the midget remote, and the car lowered to the ground. He pulled a larger remote control unit from another one of his pockets—the same remote he had used way back at the Twin Pines Mall, when this whole thing had started—and maneuvered the DeLorean in front of them.

Marty had to think. Was there anything else Doc should know?

Oh, yeah. "I think the cops said they were gonna take her home," Marty added.

"Home?" Doc frowned as he steered the remote. "Great Scott! If anyone's home who recognizes her—you, or your family—and they traumatize her . . . Or worse, if Jennifer actually encounters her future self, the consequences could be disastrous!"

Disastrous? Jennifer? Marty didn't like the sound of this.

"What do you mean?" he asked.

"The shock of coming face to face with oneself—when one is thirty years older—could be so severe that she could pass out!" Doc waved dramatically at the ground. "And if she were to fall, crack her head open, and get killed, you two certainly wouldn't be able to get married. If you don't get married, you don't have any kids. If you don't have kids, I won't have a reason to bring you both to the future in the first place, and if I don't bring you to the future, Jennifer won't get killed!"

So Jennifer would be all right, then? Marty wasn't sure he exactly understood everything the Doc had said, but that didn't sound so bad.

"Then what's the problem?" he asked.

"It creates a time paradox!" Doc waved his arms agitatedly. "A person can't be both alive and dead at the same time! It violates the laws of physics!"

Marty still didn't see the problem.

"Doc! You can't get busted for violating the laws of physics."

Doc nodded grimly. "No, but such a thing could cause a chain reaction that would unravel the very fabric of the space-time continuum and destroy the entire universe!"

He paused, considering.

"Granted," he continued, "that's a worst-case scenario. The destruction might in fact be very localized, limited to merely our own galaxy."

Only our own galaxy?

"Oh, hey, well." Marty tried to laugh. It came out more like a croak. "That's a relief."

The DeLorean pulled in front of them. Doc glanced over at what Marty was holding.

"What's in that bag?"

"This?" Marty asked innocently. Doc's gaze was awfully intense—it probably had something to do with all this talk about destroying the space-time continuum. Marty tried to shrug it off. "Oh, nothing—just a souvenir—a book that looked like it might be interesting."

Doc took the bag from Marty's hands. He pulled out the book.

"Fifty years of sports statistics," he read. "Hardly recreational reading, Marty."

"Okay, well," Marty confessed, "I figured it couldn't hurt to bring back a little info on the future. You know, in case of cash flow problems—" He was finding it a little difficult to talk under Doc's level glare. "I'd place a few bets—" His voice trailed off. He tried to smile, but Doc wasn't buying it.

"Marty," Doc replied in his best lecturer voice. "I did not invent time travel for financial gain!" He paused, book still in hand, to grab the lapels of his lab coat. "The intent here is to gain a clearer perception of humanity—where we've been, where we're going, the pitfalls and the possibilities, the perils and the promise. Perhaps even an answer to that universal question: Why?"

Doc paused to gaze nobly at the horizon. Apparently, he was finished with the lecture for the time being. But Marty still couldn't see what he was doing wrong.

"Oh, hey, I'm all for that, Doc," he replied. "But what's wrong with making a few bucks on the side?"

Doc's intense gaze once again shifted to Marty. "Because the risks far outweigh any potential rewards."

Marty had been wrong. Doc was still in lecture mode.

Doc Brown put the book back in the bag and tossed it in one of the futuristic garbage cans that lined the alley. Marty sighed. He guessed Doc was right, but it was a shame to lose that kind of opportunity. He supposed he would have to find other, more difficult ways to keep his life from the toilet.

Doc opened the gull-wing door. Someone barked. Marty looked in past the inventor's shoulder. Doc's sheep dog was in the car!

"Move over, Einstein!" Doc Brown said in the same tone he had used with Marty.

Marty circled to his side of the car and opened his own door.

"Einie!" he called. "Where did you come from, boy?" He climbed into the car next to the sheep dog, and realized he was still holding onto the hoverboard. He stuffed the flat, pink gizmo behind the passenger seat.

"I'd left Einstein here in a suspended animation kennel when I went back to 1985 to bring you here," Doc explained. "He never knew I was gone!" He reached over and ruffled the dog's fur. "We'll be home soon, boy. Just sit tight."

With the press of a button, Doc closed both of the doors and pushed the DeLorean aloft. Now all they had to do was rescue Jennifer—somehow—without destroying the fabric of the universe!

Neither Doc nor Marty thought to look behind them as the DeLorean headed for the skyway. If they had, there was a chance they might have seen the figure of an old man step out of the shadows near the alley to watch them depart. Biff Tannen.

But they wouldn't have heard what Biff muttered to himself. "So Doc Brown invented a time machine!"

They wouldn't have realized that old Biff had been listening in on the entire conversation they'd just had.

They wouldn't have seen Biff reach into a certain trash can and fish out a silver bag with a certain sports almanac in it.

And they wouldn't have seen him hail a flying taxi.

Fred saw the old fellow waving his brass-handled cane as the cabbie let out his last fare. The parrot on his shoulder squawked.

"What's the matter, Priscilla?" he asked the bird. "Don't you think we should pick this guy up?"

"Taxi!" the old guy yelled.

The parrot squawked a second time.

Fred shook his head as he eased the taxi forward. "Sorry, Priscilla. A fare is a fare."

The old man scrambled into the backseat of the cab, muttering something about "two hick flies" or something like that. Maybe, Fred thought, this guy was a weirdo, after all.

The oldster pointed a quivering finger at a sleek silver car that was just taking off overhead.

"Follow that DeLorean!" he croaked.

Follow that DeLorean? That was the sort of thing people said in old, 2-D movies! Where was this old guy coming from?

Still, a fare was a fare. Fred eased the cab out and up.

The old guy kept muttering something about "time" and "he'd show them!" and stuff like that. Yep. He was a definite weirdo.

Fred sighed. After all this time, he should have known enough to trust his parrot.

• Chapter
Six •

Officer Foley had to admit it. There were some parts of her job she liked a lot less than others. And taking tranks and addicts home had to be on the bottom of her list. She scanned the street as they landed. Hard to believe this neighborhood had once been a nice place to live.

"Hilldale!" Her partner, Reese, spat the name out in disgust. "They ought to tear this whole place down. Nothing more than a breeding ground for tranks, lo-bos, and zipheads."

At least, Foley thought, she and Reese agreed on something for a change. Sometimes, her partner's fanaticism about rules and regulations got to her. According to Reese, everything and anything had to be done by the book. *Stop for coffee and doughnuts? See Section 8, subparagraph C.* Reese had been a cop so long that all her human feelings were gone. Maybe, Foley reflected, she would end up like Reese, too, one of these days, her emotions buried under years of working slag-heaps like Hilldale.

Foley and Reese picked up the woman between them. She looked so young, Foley kept wanting to think of her as a girl. She must have spent a bundle at one of those cosmetic factories. And she lived in a place like this. Foley wondered if there might be something else going on here, the sort of thing a good police officer should investigate.

But she didn't even mention her thoughts to her partner. She already knew what Reese would say. *Pure conjecture, Foley. There's no place in police procedure for conjecture.* And Foley knew they didn't have time to investigate, either. They were too busy dealing with tranks and lo-bos.

They pulled the girl—woman—from the car and carried her across what passed for a lawn, putting her down on the doorstep. Foley decided they might as well get this over with. She rang the doorbell. They waited for a moment in silence. There didn't seem to be anybody home. She noticed a thumb plate by the door.

"They've got identipad," she said to her partner, pointing at the plate. "We could just take her in."

"Are you kirgo?" Reese asked with a harsh laugh. "That's a violation of the privacy act! We could get our crags numped!" She shook her head in that brusque, official way she had. "If we can't revive her, we leave her here."

Leave her out here? On the doorstep? Someone looking as young and innocent as that? In Hilldale, now, while dusk was falling? Foley hoped it wouldn't come to that.

Sometimes she hated her job.

Reese gently but firmly patted the sleeping woman's face.

"Miss? Miss?"

The woman started to come around. She blinked her eyes, having obvious trouble focusing on anything. Not at all unusual for a trank.

"Uhhh," she groaned. "Where am I?"

"You're home, Miss," Reese replied matter-of-factly. "You got a little tranked, but everything's fine. Can you walk?"

The citizen still seemed a little disoriented.

"I—I don't know," she managed after a moment.

"Would you like us to take you inside?" Reese asked.

Foley was surprised at that. She guessed, once the citizen was awake, regulations would allow you to offer assistance. Or maybe her partner still had some human feelings, after all.

"Oohhh—" The woman's eyes almost crossed. Foley guessed she would have trouble standing, much less walking. "Okay," the citizen added weakly.

So now they could use the identiplate. Sometimes, Foley swore, she could make no sense at all out of those numping regulations! Foley gently picked up the citizen's limp hand and pressed the woman's thumb into the plate below the doorbell. The door whooshed open.

Reese and Foley each took one of the woman's arms and helped her inside.

"Welcome home, Jennifer!" a computer voice chirruped merrily. No surprise that the computer was one of those outdated models, all warm and insincere.

Since the lights didn't come on, there was no way to tell where they were going. They took her into what should have been the living room.

"Ma'am," Reese spoke with as much concern as Foley had ever heard. "You should reprogram. It's dangerous to enter without lights on."

"Lights on?" the citizen replied groggily.

The computer activated the lights at the voice command. Voice activation? This program was even older than Foley had imagined!

And the furniture in this place! She was sure there wasn't anything in here made after 1990. The scratched coffee table, sagging couches, and threadbare chairs, all reminded Foley of the kind of stuff you'd find in one of those charity stores—except the stuff in those stores would be in a lot better shape.

The two officers eased the citizen down on the sofa.

"Just take it easy and you'll be fine," Reese said brusquely. "And you be careful in the future."

The citizen—Jennifer—looked groggily up at the two officers.

"The future?"

There was the oddest expression on her face—like there was something wrong with the future. Maybe, Foley thought, she was just reading into the woman's expression. Still, it wasn't surprising. When you lived in a place like Hilldale, you didn't have much of a future to look forward to.

"So long, Mrs. McFly," Foley called, trying to sound cheerful despite it all.

"So long," the citizen replied, still half in her tranked-out stupor. In a way, Foley couldn't blame her for turning to chemicals. Who knew—maybe Foley would have done the same thing if she had been stuck in a dead-end place like this?

Reese headed for the door. Foley hurried to follow.

The door whooshed closed behind them, and they were back out on the rough streets of Hilldale.

Foley felt empty, deep in her stomach.

Sometimes, she really hated this job.

"Mrs. McFly!"

Jennifer woke up. That's what the police officers had called her. Mrs. McFly. And they had talked to her about the future. Was that where she was? The future? She remembered getting in the DeLorean with Marty and Doc, the lights and noise, and then that display that said they were in 2015. That's right! She had been all excited about being here with Marty, and had started asking Doc Brown all those questions.

And then what?

She must have fallen asleep. But how could you fall asleep if you had just gone someplace as exciting as the future? And why wasn't she in the DeLorean anymore? Had something happened to Marty and Doc? It must have. They wouldn't just leave her all alone—would they? And why had she been with the police?

And where had the police left her?

She stood up and looked around. The policewomen had called her *Mrs*. McFly. Could this be where she lived—in the future?

The first thing she noticed was a large picture window that looked out over the grounds of what must be a very large estate. There were manicured lawns, formal gardens, and row after row of neatly trimmed hedges, all leading back to a charming white gazebo in the distance. The view was all quite lovely, except for one thing. It was daylight out there. Hadn't it been getting dark a few minutes ago, when the cops brought her in?

Jennifer frowned as she looked at the room around her. Shouldn't the furniture be nicer if they lived in a mansion? The things she could see, in this room at least, looked pretty shabby. There were stairs going up to the second floor at one end of the living room, right next to the front door. She wondered if she should go upstairs to see if things were any different.

She glanced over at a bookcase that took up most of the wall next to the stairs. There was *A Match Made in Space*, the book Marty's father had written!

Jennifer walked over to get a closer look, and saw that it wasn't a book, after all; the label on its side said "videobook", whatever that was. And just beyond that on the shelf were another half-dozen videobooks, all of them with neatly hand-written labels:

FAMILY VACATIONS—1995-2005
GEORGE & LORRAINE 50TH ANNIVERSARY
THE KIDS: MARTY JUNIOR AND MARLENE, VOL. I
THE KIDS: MARTY JUNIOR AND MARLENE, VOL. 3
THE KIDS: MARTY JUNIOR AND MARLENE, VOL. 2

Jennifer gasped. This really was her house that the police had brought her to—her house in the future, that is. This wasn't just any old future, it was *her* future.

But all thoughts of the videobooks left her when she took a closer look at the framed photo at the end of the shelf. It was a wedding picture—of Jennifer and Marty. But she was just wearing everyday clothes, and Marty was wearing a T-shirt with a tux front printed on it! What had happened to that big church wedding that she had wanted? They were both standing in front of a big neon sign that read "Las Vegas's own CHAPEL OF LOVE!" Chapel of Love? They must have eloped!

"Oh, my God!" Jennifer cried. "I get married in the Chapel of Love?"

She and Marty had eloped? What about their parents? What could have happened to their future?

A girl's voice called out from upstairs.

"Mom? Is that you?"

Oh, no. There was somebody else here! What could Jennifer do?

"I've gotta get out of here!" she whispered. The wedding photo fell from her hands and clattered to the floor. She ran for the front door as she heard footsteps upstairs.

Jennifer stopped and stared at the door in horror. There was no doorknob. There were no marks of any kind, only some weird metal plate on the wall nearby. The front door was nothing but a solid slab of wood. She stepped up to the door and pushed against it. It didn't budge. How could she possibly get it open?

Jennifer jumped as the doorbell rang. There must be somebody on the other side of the front door, somebody right in front of her. Maybe the newcomer knew the secret way to open this thing. What if the front door suddenly disappeared or something? But Jennifer didn't want to be seen, by anybody! She turned around, looking for some other way out of here. The footsteps upstairs were getting louder. She thought she saw the girl's shadow on the landing.

"Mom?" the girl called. "Mom?"

Where could Jennifer go?

•Chapter
Seven•

Jennifer spotted a louvered door beyond the bookcase, a door with a handle that she could open and close. Maybe it was a way out of here!

She yanked the door open, and was confronted by a dozen hanging coats.

She heard the footsteps start down the stairs overhead.

Jennifer jumped into the closet. She eased the door shut behind her. The footsteps clumped heavily toward the front door. Who could it be? If this was her house, in her future, would it be someone in her family? Jennifer wished she could see what was going on out there.

Maybe she could. There was light coming into the closet from the louvered door. She shifted around as quietly as possible, doing her best to keep the coats behind her. If she leaned forward just so, she could peek through the slats.

A teenage girl stepped into the living room at the bottom of the stairs. Oh, my God! Jennifer breathed in sharply. The teenager was the spitting image of Marty!

The teenager disappeared from sight as she moved toward the front door. There was a soft whooshing sound.

The teenager stepped back into view. "Oh, hi, Grandma Lorraine."

Grandma Lorraine? Marty's mother? Jennifer peeked through the slats, but the newcomer was still out of sight.

"Hi, sweetheart," Grandma Lorraine replied. She sounded like Marty's mother. "I brought dinner. Are your folks home yet?"

The teenager shrugged her broad shoulders. She was built sort of huskily for a girl, Jennifer thought, probably one of those high school athletic types.

"Mom should be home any minute," the teenager answered her grandmother. "Dad—who knows?"

"Mom?" Jennifer asked under her breath.

She blinked. If Dad was Marty . . .

Oh my God! Jennifer realized—it would have been obvious if this future business wasn't all so new to her—she was Mom!

The teenager stepped back to let her grandmother in. Grandma Lorraine walked past the stairs, so Jennifer could see her at last. She *was* Marty's mother, older now, with gray hair. Still, she looked pretty good for a woman in her seventies. She was carrying a small, silver bag—too small, Jennifer thought, to hold dinner for a whole family. So where was the food?

"Grandpa!" the teenage girl called. "You threw your back out again!"

There was a humming noise as a machine coasted across Jennifer's view, a machine that held Marty's father—with gray hair now, but still as skinny as ever—strapped in *upside down*! George stopped the gizmo right in front of the bookcase next to Jennifer's hiding place, close enough for her to read the "Ortho-lev" nameplate on the machine's crossbar.

"Your grandpa got hit by a car," Grandma Lorraine explained. "On the golf course! It just dropped out of the sky. He could have been killed!" She shook her head with a grandmotherly frown. "I don't know what this world's coming to."

"I'll take this, Grandma."

The teenage girl—boy, did she look like Marty!—stepped in front of Jennifer's hiding place and took the little bag from Lorraine.

Grandma Lorraine walked over to the window. There seemed to be something wrong with the view now. The lawn, the gardens, the gazebo—all of it was slowly rolling, like a TV screen that was losing its vertical hold. There was also snow or static or something up toward the top of the picture.

"Oh." Grandma spoke as if she wasn't surprised. "This window's *still* broken."

She walked back across the room and picked up

a remote control unit from the bookshelf. The image in the window changed to a tropical island, then abruptly shifted to a mountain view, and just as quickly changed to a picture of a city at night, but all three flipped and were full of static. Then the city, too, blipped out of existence, replaced a moment later by a nighttime view that was nowhere near as picturesque.

This, Jennifer realized, must be the real view outside, with no flip, and no static. It showed the side of the building next door, complete with half a dozen garbage cans overflowing with trash.

"Maybe we should buy them a new one," Grandma Lorraine suggested. "What do you think, George? We could afford it."

She stepped farther into the room, out of Jennifer's line of sight.

"Well . . ." Grandpa George didn't sound very enthusiastic. Or very quick to make up his mind.

"I don't know," he said at last. His floating harness whirred as he picked something up from the floor. Jennifer's heart almost stopped when she realized it was the wedding photo she had dropped! But old George merely put the photo back on its shelf—although Jennifer could have sworn he put the picture back upside down.

"Yeah, Grandma," the teenage girl spoke again. Seeing Lorraine fiddle with that big video screen reminded Jennifer about the names written on those videobooks—the ones about the kids. Marty Junior and—Marlene?

"You know Dad," Marlene went on about her grandmother's offer. "He'd probably get, like, pissquanced."

"Pissquanced?" Grandma asked with a distasteful frown.

"You know, insulted," Marlene answered. "He'd think that, well—"

Her grandmother nodded, suddenly understanding.

"That we were reminding him that he can't afford it?" She sighed as if she had heard this story over and over again. "Poor Marty. He's always been so concerned about what people think about him, what they say about him behind his back." She glanced at her upside-down husband. "How many times have we heard it, George? 'Mom, I can't let 'em think I'm cheap! I can't let 'em think I'm not with it! I can't let 'em think I'm chicken!' "

Lorraine and Marlene walked past Jennifer's hiding place, then turned past the living room sofa to go into the back of the house, as Grandpa George once again started up his machine.

Jennifer looked beyond them, through the doorway.

There, at the very back of the house, was another door, with another doorknob. It might be a way out. At the very least, it was better than being stuck in the closet. Jennifer bit her lip. Should she?

She opened the closet door. The three others were busy talking as they moved away from her. Maybe, if Jennifer moved quietly enough, she could get over to those other doors without anybody noticing. It was worth a try. She really couldn't stay in this closet forever. And, as she snuck past them, she could still hear what they had to say. After all, they were talking about Marty's future, and her future, too!

Jennifer crept from her hiding place.

"You're right . . ." Grandpa George slowly answered his wife.

Grandma Lorraine sighed again. "About thirty years ago Marty decided to *prove* he wasn't chicken—and he ended up in an automobile accident."

Thirty years ago? Jennifer frowned. That would be back in 1985, wouldn't it? But nothing like that had happened to Marty. At least, it hadn't happened yet.

"Oh, you mean with the Rolls Royce?" Marlene asked matter-of-factly. "You're garbed on that, Grandma. That wasn't Dad's fault. He told me so himself."

Jennifer tiptoed out into the open. The three others had paused at the entryway to what seemed to be the kitchen. In a minute, she figured, they'd walk into that room. Then she would have a clear path to that back door, and a way out of here.

"And what does your mother say?" Grandma insisted. "She was there, too, you know."

Your mother?

Jennifer stopped moving. She had been there, too—with Marty? What could have happened? Or what—she reminded herself—was going to happen?

Marlene shrugged her broad shoulders.

"Mom's never talked about it."

Grandma Lorraine wagged her index finger at Marlene.

"Well, the truth is, if your father had just used a little common sense, that accident would have never happened. That accident started a chain reaction that sent Marty's life straight down the tubes!"

"Now, Lorraine . . ." Grandpa George chided slowly.

Jennifer couldn't believe what Marty's mother was saying. Marty wouldn't do something like that, just because he'd hit somebody's car—would he? Jennifer had married someone whose life had gone down the tubes?

"George," Lorraine insisted, "she might as well know the truth." Her finger wagged at Marlene one more time. "If not for that accident, your father's life would have turned out very differently. The man in the Rolls Royce wouldn't have pressed charges or sued him, Marty wouldn't have broken his hand, he wouldn't have given up on his music, and he wouldn't have spent all those years feeling sorry for himself, complaining how life gave him such a raw deal." She made a clucking sound with her tongue against her teeth. "He wouldn't have just given up on life."

Marlene rolled her eyes upward, as if she didn't want to hear all this. But Grandpa George nodded his head in agreement.

"You're right . . ." he said slowly. "You're right."

Grandma turned back to Marlene again. "The real reason your mother married him was because she felt sorry for him. Such a sweet girl. She deserved better."

Jennifer deserved better? Marty's life had gone down the tubes? They had gotten married in the Chapel of Love? But Marty was such a sweet guy! How could the future turn out this way? Jennifer didn't like the sound of any of this!

There was a great clatter overhead. Jennifer froze. Someone was coming down the stairs, fast.

But Jennifer was in the middle of the living room. There was nowhere she could hide. She was right out in the open!

Before she could think what to do, Marty Junior jumped into view.

"Hi, Mom!" Junior called as he ran past her, following the other three, who had all finally gone through the door into the kitchen.

Oh brother, Jennifer thought with relief. Marty Junior—who also looked remarkably like his father—hadn't even looked at her! Lucky for her, he paid as much attention to most things as his father did!

The cheerful computer voice rumbled to life.

"Welcome home, Marty, oh master of the house, king of the castle, lord of the manor!"

The computer greeting—that must mean that Marty Senior was coming home!

She heard another noise behind her—a soft,

whooshing noise—the same sound she had heard the last time the front door opened. And she was still in the middle of the room!

There was another door, half open, at the far end of the living room. She jumped inside. She glanced behind her long enough to see she was in a bathroom—not all that different from bathrooms she knew. She quickly closed the door behind her, leaving just enough space for her to peek out.

Her heart almost stopped when she saw who walked through the living room, heading toward the kitchen. It was Marty Senior, *her* Marty, decked out in a business suit—although for some reason he was wearing two ties. But he looked so much older, so much grayer. Could he have changed this much in thirty years?

"Hi, everybody," he called as he walked into the kitchen, out of Jennifer's view. "I'm home!"

Maybe, she thought, she should get out of here herself. But where could she go? She turned around at last to get a good look at this bathroom.

Wait a minute. This bathroom had another door, right behind her back! She was lucky that no one had walked in while she had been looking out the other way.

She turned to the second door and cautiously opened it a crack, and found herself looking into the kitchen.

Grandfather George waved from his harness.

"Hi, son . . ."

Marty Senior grinned at his parents.

"Hey, Dad, how're you feeling? How's the back?"

"Okay . . ." his father answered after a moment's thought.

Lorraine stepped forward with that sweet, motherly smile of hers.

"How are things at work, Marty?" she asked gently.

Marty shrugged and sighed.

"Oh, same old, same old."

So everyone was in the kitchen. Jennifer realized that maybe now she could leave through the other door and get out of this place without anybody seeing her.

She turned back to the door she'd entered through, and realized, as soon as she looked through the crack she'd left there, that everybody wasn't in the room beyond. Marty Junior stood in the next room, calling out numbers at a big screen. The screen responded by showing different pictures for six different television programs. The thing Marty Junior was watching was some sort of giant, multichannel video screen—a screen that hung crooked on the wall. Jennifer had to push back an urge to rush out there and try to straighten the picture out.

Marty Senior walked into the room behind his son. He picked up a pile of papers from a basket and quickly sorted through them. "Ah," he muttered to himself. "Nothin' but junk fax!"

He turned to his son. "Junior! Dinnertime!"

Junior didn't budge.

"But I'm watching TV!" he shouted over his shoulder.

"Well, get your glasses," Marty Senior insisted. "We eat at the table when your grandparents are here."

Junior got up as slowly as he could.

"Aw, Dad," he whined, "I can only watch two shows at once on my glasses!"

Marty Senior laughed and shook his head. "Yeah, you kids really have it tough! When I was your age, if I wanted to watch two shows at once, I had to put two sets next to each other!"

Marty Junior didn't seem impressed. He wandered back toward the kitchen. His father straightened the video screens, adding, "Let's have some art, please!"

The six TV programs disappeared, replaced by what looked like a very large, bright painting of a bowl of fruit! Marty Senior turned and followed his son from the room.

Jennifer realized the whole family was going to sit down to dinner, all in one place, out of sight of the bathroom door. There probably wouldn't be a better time for her to get out of here.

But—even if that other door led outside—where would she go? She didn't know anything at all about the future! What had happened to Marty and Doc, anyway? How could she possibly find them?

For the first time, Jennifer realized she might be lost in the future for good.

If only it wasn't too late!

Doc Brown steered the car into Hilldale, a once-fashionable section of town that—to put it mildly—had seen better days.

The cops, after identifying Jennifer from her thumbprint, would have brought her here—to the McFly place. It was standard police procedure. What wouldn't have been standard was whatever happened to Jennifer after she got here—especially if an older, 2015 version of that same Jennifer had been at home. The implications . . .

Doc Brown didn't want to think about those implications. This whole thing had gotten far too complicated already.

Doc looked over at his passenger as he landed the car. Marty was all smiles, turning quickly from the front windshield to the side window and back again, trying to see as much as he could in the darkness.

"So I live in Hilldale?" he bubbled. "Great! They just *built* it! Everybody says it's a real hip place to live." He shook his fist victoriously. "Way to go, McFly!"

Doc didn't have the heart to tell Marty about what happened to the neighborhood. The less Marty knew about the future, the better.

Doc set down the car around the corner from the McFly place—near enough to do the job quickly, but not so close as to be conspicuous.

Now all he needed was Einstein's nose, and a little luck, and they could keep those implications he wouldn't think about from getting any worse. He opened his gull-wing door and climbed from the car, then turned to fish behind his seat for Jennifer's purse, which, fortuitously, had been left behind in the car.

Ah! There it was, right behind that hoverboard Marty had picked up somewhere. He pulled the purse out and stuck it under Einstein's nose.

"All right, Einie, pick up Jennifer's scent."

The dog snuffled the purse.

"You got it?"

The dog barked enthusiastically.

"Good!" Doc Brown smiled. "Let's find her."

He looked over at his eager teenage sidekick. There was one more thing that needed to be taken care of.

Doc pointed to the car. "Marty, stay here. Change clothes. If I need you, I'll holler."

Marty stared back at him, openmouthed.

"But, Doc—"

Doc cut off Marty's protest before he could begin.

"We can't risk you running into yourself," he said firmly. "C'mon, Einie."

Einstein jumped from the car and ran straight toward the McFly house. Good! That meant Jennifer had to be inside. With luck, he and his dog could get in there, grab the young lady, and get out in a matter of seconds. If not . . .

Doc sighed softly and headed for the house. There wasn't any time for "if nots." There was only time to get the job done, before things got even more complicated.

• • •

So this was Hilldale?

Marty had gotten excited as soon as he had seen the twin signs by the entrance: HILLDALE—THE ADDRESS OF SUCCESS.

But here they were, in this classy place, and Doc had told him to stay with the DeLorean and change his clothes!

Marty pulled off his future hat, jacket, and shoes, and fished in the gym bag for his regular 1985 clothes. He pulled out his sneakers first, put them on, and knelt down to tie them. He missed the power laces already.

A dog barked behind him. Marty glanced back, and saw a dog and a leash with nobody on the other end. The leash was just sort of hanging up there in the air. Of course! Marty thought. It must be some kind of automatic dog-walker. Wow, the future!

The dog trotted obediently around the corner—the same corner Doc had taken a minute before. Maybe, Marty considered, now that he had his shoes on and all, maybe he should take a closer look at that dog, and, maybe, whatever else might be around the corner, like his future house. Sure, like Doc said, maybe it was dangerous to know too much about your future, but—hey—he already knew he lived here. What could it hurt if he went and took a little stroll?

Marty dumped the gym bag in the back of the DeLorean and trotted around the corner.

If only Marty hadn't been so curious about his own future, what was about to happen might never have happened. Even if Marty had merely looked behind him before starting forward, it might have been prevented. Because if Marty had looked behind him, he might have seen the flying taxi coming down, the same flying taxi that old Biff Tannen had flagged down a little while ago. Perhaps Marty might have seen old Biff in that flying taxi. But Marty didn't look behind him. He walked forward toward his future residence. And that would prove to be a serious mistake.

"There!" the old guy yelled from the backseat. "Up there!"

Fred glanced over his shoulder to see the old guy pointing straight ahead. Fred turned back to look at the road. Yeah, there was the parked DeLorean. There was a kid kneeling in front of it, putting on a pair of shoes. At least, that's what it looked like the kid was doing. Fred wondered how many cars got stolen every night in a place like Hilldale?

Well, Fred guessed, he was glad they found the car again. The taxi driver had thought the old guy in the back was going to have a heart attack when he had stopped the cab outside Hilldale. Fred didn't really like to go into this kind of neighborhood, especially after dark. But, with a choice of getting a fare or having a dead guy in his backseat, Fred had decided to make an exception in this case, and had taken the cab into Hilldale.

Lucky for the old guy's continuing health, the DeLorean hadn't gotten very far ahead. Fred pulled up next to it as the old guy shouted, "You can let me off here!"

Fred noticed that the kid had disappeared. Maybe the teenager had really been doing something to his shoes, after all.

The taxi driver glanced at the meter.

"That'll be $174.40."

The parrot on his shoulder squawked. "Nope! $174.50!"

Fred glanced back at the meter. Priscilla was right.

"Oh yeah," he amended, "that's $174.50. And I'd be careful in this neighborhood, old-timer."

But the old guy didn't want to listen. He hastily pressed his thumb to the payment plate, then scrambled from the cab. He moved with amazing speed for somebody his age as he hobbled with the aid of his cane toward the DeLorean, a silver bag clutched in his free hand.

He walked straight to the car, opened the door, and climbed inside.

What was the old guy doing? Was that his car? Fred decided he didn't want to know. He turned the cab around and headed out of Hilldale.

Priscilla squawked chidingly in his ear, and Fred had to agree.

After all this time, why hadn't he learned to listen to his parrot?

•Chapter Eight•

He wished his wife would get home. She *knew* Marty's mother and father were going to be here tonight, but she was still off on one of her little errands. Nump! If both their teenaged children could get home in time for the grandparents, was it too much to ask for their mother to show up, too?

In the meantime, Marty's mother was bustling around the food processors, getting everything ready for dinner. Grandma Lorraine always took over like this whenever Jennifer wasn't here, which seemed to happen far too often recently. Where, Marty wondered, had he and Jennifer gone wrong?

Grandma Lorraine stuck one of those expandable pizzas in the hydrator—a real four-incher! That was one thing you could say about Marty McFly Senior's parents: They weren't cheap.

"So I thought," she continued cheerily as she distributed the plates, "it would be nice if we threw a little party for him."

The hydrator beeped. His mother bustled happily back to the machine, pulling the now fifteen-inch pizza free. And she was nice enough not to mention it had taken the hydrator a full twelve-second cycle to finish their dinner. Marty wished he could afford one of those new six-second models.

But, as nice as his mother was, there were still a few things that she just couldn't be realistic about. Like this party she kept going on about.

"Mom," Marty Senior replied patiently, "before we throw a party for Uncle Joey, let's see if he makes parole."

"Fumble!" Junior screamed. The readout on his glasses read: ESPN—Ch 211-D. He must be watching the Spacers/Bears game.

Grandma Lorraine brought the steaming pizza to the table.

"George," she added gently, "rotate your axis, please. It's not good for your digestion to eat while you're inverted."

Marty's father obediently pushed a button by his wrist. The ortho rig whirred into action, turning him sideways.

"I can't believe it!" Junior yelled.

It must be a good game. The Bears were finally showing the rest of the IFL that they were no longer has-beens. They were having their best season in almost thirty years! Marty Senior half-wished he could watch the game himself.

Grandma Lorraine sat down at the table. The pizza looked great. They'd have a real family dinner for a change, Marty thought, even though Jennifer *still* wasn't home.

"Pass the kelp tea, please," Marty asked his daughter.

Marlene pouted behind her own set of vidglasses.

"No," she whined, "I don't want to, so nump off!"

"Take him out of the game!" Junior pounded his fists on the table.

"Marlene!" Grandma Lorraine reprimanded sharply. "Don't talk to your father like that!"

"Grandma!" Marlene barked, pointing at the word and number display on her vidglasses. "I'm on the phone, okay?" Marty's daughter looked away, long-suffering, as if no teenager should ever have to put up with this sort of thing.

Somebody's beeper started to chatter as red lights went off on both of the kid's vidglasses. Marty looked down at the flashing light in his pocket.

It was *his* beeper.

"Dad!" Junior and Marlene yelled together. "Telephone! It's Needles!"

Marty stood up and flipped off his signal. Suddenly his throat was very dry. He felt like everybody at the dinner table was watching him—even the kids behind their vidglasses. If this call was what he thought it was, he'd need a little privacy.

"I'll take it in the den." He walked from the room, sliding the door closed behind him.

He paused a minute as he passed the mirror to straighten his ties and make sure his hair was combed. This was a serious decision he had to make. It might change his whole future—for the better, Marty hoped. Maybe he could make things up to Jennifer, give her all those things she should have gotten. If only this deal were a little more straight-forward ... Marty stopped himself with a final check in the mirror. When Needles talked with him on the vidphone, he wanted to look his best.

He walked quickly in front of the video screen.

What was that? He blinked and shook his head.

For a second there, he thought he had seen something out of the corner of his eye. In fact, he could have sworn that Jennifer had been peeking at him around the edge of the bathroom door. He was so nervous, he must be imagining things.

He picked up the remote control and banished the art channel painting to the corner of the screen.

Needles smiled his gap-toothed grin as his head and shoulders filled the rest of the video display and his identification code flashed on: NEEDLES, DOUGLAS J. ADDRESS: 88 ORIOLE RD. A6TB-94. That was his home address; not that Needles was ever home. From the row of vidmemos behind him, Marty could tell the other man was still at his station at work. Sometimes Marty wondered if Needles ever left the office.

"Hey, the Big M!" Needles began boisterously. "How's it hangin', McFly?"

"Hey, Needles," Marty replied, trying not to sound nervous.

Needles didn't seem to notice. Instead, he launched quickly into exactly what Marty had to do if their little plan was going to work. Somehow, whenever Needles explained this sort of thing—in all the years they had known each other, ever since high school—it always sounded so easy.

"So what do you say, Marty?" he finished breezily, once more flashing the grin that had gotten Needles to a position in the organization that Marty could never hope to reach.

Marty opened his mouth, but no noise came out. Despite all the things he wanted, he was having a real hard time saying yes.

"I—" he managed at last. "Uh—"

"McFly!" Needles insisted. "What are you afraid of? If this thing works, it'll solve all your financial problems."

"And if it doesn't work, I could get fired!" Marty retorted, finding his voice at last. There was one thing his co-worker forgot to mention, something Marty had to get out in the open. "It's *illegal*, Needles."

Marty had another thought. Needles was calling from the office. Everybody knew the way their boss was with personal calls!

"What if the Jits is monitoring?" Marty asked, his voice suddenly hushed.

Needles looked Marty straight in the screen.

"The Jits will never find out. Come on, just stick your card in the slot and I'll handle it. Unless you want everyone in the division to think you're—" Needles paused ominously—"chicken."

Chicken?

The screen suddenly appeared to turn red before Marty's eyes. Blood rushed in his ears; his heart jackhammered in his chest.

Chicken?

He spat out the words from between clenched teeth:

"Nobody calls me chicken!"

Needles nodded curtly, his grin even broader than before.

"All right," he said to Marty. "Prove it."

That was it! He'd show Needles. He'd show Jennifer and his kids and his parents and everybody who ever thought he was a failure. He'd show everybody! He whipped out his wallet and pulled free his card.

"Here," he almost shouted, plugging his card into the slot in his briefcase as the lights along the side flashed his personal code. "Scan it! I'm in."

Needles did just that. Marty heard a quick series of electronic tones as his bar codes were recorded on the deal.

"Thanks, McFly," Needles said, the easy grin once again in place. "See you at the plant tomorrow."

Needles cut the connection. The screen went blank.

Marty took a deep breath. Well, that was that. He hadn't really meant to go along; there were all these complications that the rest of the guys had sort of ignored. But Needles had called him chicken—nobody called him chicken!—and he was in.

His card had been scanned and put on record. There was no turning back—and maybe Needles was right. Maybe his future road was paved with gold.

He pressed the remote, flipping the art channel so that it once again filled the screen. Marty felt exhausted. All he wanted to do now was get back into the other room and finish his dinner.

He turned away from the video screen.

"McFly!" a voice rumbled behind him.

It was the last voice in the world Marty wanted to hear. This had to be a coincidence. Didn't it?

He turned back to the screen and the full-sized image of his glowering boss.

"Mr. Fujitsu, sir!" Marty did his best to smile. "Good evening, sir!"

The boss stared at Marty for a moment; the large man seething silently. Maybe it was the formal dress kimono that his boss liked to wear in the evenings, but whenever Fujitsu got like this, he always reminded Marty of a meditating samurai warrior just before he went on a killing rampage.

Marty realized his throat had gone dry all over again.

"McFly," Fujitsu said slowly and all-too-clearly,

"I was monitoring that scan you just interfaced. *You're terminated!*"

No! His boss couldn't mean that!

"Terminated?" Marty protested. "But sir! It wasn't my idea! Needles was behind it!" Surely, his boss could see the truth in that.

"And you cooperated," Fujitsu continued, unswayed by Marty's argument. "It was illegal, and you knew it." The boss's voice was growing quieter. It was always worse when an angry Fujitsu got quiet. Marty could almost feel that samurai sword slicing through his future.

"You're fired, McFly," Fujitsu concluded calmly. "Good-bye."

Fired? Just like that?

"But sir—" Marty began rapidly. It wasn't his fault. There had to be some way to get the boss to see that. Needles had called Marty chicken! *Nobody* called Marty chicken!

"McFly!" Fujitsu cut him off abruptly. "Read my fax!"

The boss's face disappeared from the screen, replaced by a piece of company stationery, addressed to Marty McFly Senior. Besides the address, and Fujitsu's signature on the bottom, there were only two words on that piece of paper.

YOU'RE FIRED!

Fired?

Marty could hear the soft whir of the fax unit on the other side of the den as it printed out the facsimile copy of the message on the screen.

And Fujitsu was gone. He had broken the connection. The art channel once again filled the screen.

Marty could almost feel the sword in his heart. His future was over.

Jennifer jumped as a machine whirred by her elbow.

She glanced over at the piece of paper the machine spat out, a piece of paper filled mostly with two very large words:

YOU'RE FIRED!

Jennifer picked up the sheet of paper. This must be the fax that the muscular Japanese fellow had been talking about on the TV screen. And it printed this paper in the bathroom? Jennifer wondered if there were machines like this in every room of the house.

"Jennifer!"

She jumped again as the voice whispered her name behind her. She crumpled the paper and thrust it in her pocket, whirling around to see who had called her.

There, looking in the bathroom window, was Doc Brown!

Doc Brown? Jennifer had never been so happy to see a scientist in her entire life!

"Go out the front door!" Doc Brown whispered urgently. "I'll meet you there!"

Jennifer frowned, her happiness once again drowned in a sea of confusion. Out the front door? But, how could she get out the front door?

"It won't open!" she complained. "There's no doorknob!"

Doc nodded as if it was only now that he understood.

"Press your thumb to the plate!" he explained.

Oh. Jennifer remembered that funny-looking plate at the side of the front door. So that's how it worked.

But that meant she could finally get out of here.

Jennifer nodded to Doc. She stepped across the bathroom and looked out through the door she had entered. There was no one in either of the rooms she could see. She pushed opened the bathroom door and crept as quietly as she could toward the front door.

She heard Grandma Lorraine loudly complaining behind her, "Marty, what's the meaning of this fax?"

"Believe me, Mom, it wasn't my fault," Marty Senior explained, a slight whine to his voice. "I just always seem to get a raw deal on everything!"

At least, Jennifer hoped, if the family was busy arguing, they wouldn't even look her way as she snuck out of the house. Now, all she had to do was find the—what had Doc Brown called it?—oh yeah, the thumb plate.

There, next to the front door, was another fax machine, with another paper saying: YOU'RE FIRED! Jennifer realized they really *did* have these machines all over the house. And right beyond the machine was the metal plate she was looking for.

She reached her hand forward, ready to press her thumb to the middle of the plate.

"Welcome home, Jennifer!" the computer boomed cheerily.

Wait a moment. Should the computer be welcoming her when she was going out?

The door opened before she could put her thumb on the plate.

There was a woman standing in the doorway. A woman who looked an awful lot like her, only puffier, with more wrinkles, and dark circles under her eyes.

Jennifer realized she was looking at her older self.

"Oh, my God!" she screamed. "I'm *old*!"

After that, everything went black.

While Doc, Marty, and Jennifer were busy at the house, none of them saw Biff take off in the De-Lorean, or, a moment later, land the DeLorean in the exact same spot. He quickly got out to hobble away, too quickly, maybe, because his cane got caught as the gull-wing door swung down. The cane snapped in two as Biff struggled with it. He took the half he had freed and hobbled away, leaving everything like it was before—except that now Biff no longer clutched the silver bag.

•Chapter
Nine•

It was every bit as bad as Doc Brown thought it would be. A second after the two Jennifers spotted each other, both of them had fainted dead away.

There was a little luck involved, though. Both of them had also fallen forward—the 2015 Jennifer into the house, and the 1985 version out onto the front steps. And Doc had been there to catch her, and pull her all the way outside so that the door would close behind her. That part was neat, if Doc thought so himself. Now all he had to do was maneuver the unconscious Jennifer back to the car, and they could get out of here!

As he steered the dead weight in his arms down the steps, he could hear Marty Senior's voice through the door.

"Looks like your mother's tranked again!"

Doc sighed. Well, maybe Marty Senior and Jennifer didn't have the happiest life in 2015, but there was nothing Doc Brown could do about it. He didn't dare tamper any more with their lives, in the past or the future! This fiasco with Jennifer had convinced him just how dangerous time traveling could be!

Doc stopped to catch his breath. Jennifer weighed down Doc's arms until they were almost numb, and he had barely managed to drag her twenty feet! Doc never realized how heavy an unconscious seventeen-year-old girl could be. He saw his young sidekick running up the walk, and decided he could use some help.

"Marty!" he called. "Come quick!"

Marty looked terribly afraid as he ran up to the two of them.

"Is she alive?" he whispered as he looked down at Jennifer.

"She's in shock," Doc answered hurriedly, "as I predicted, but otherwise she seems unhurt. Let's get her back to 1985, and then I'm going to destroy the time machine."

Marty looked up at Doc, the fear turned to surprise.

"Destroy it? But what about all that stuff about humanity, finding out where we're going, and why?"

Doc shook his head firmly. It had been a tough decision, but he wouldn't go back on it now.

"The risks are just too great—as this incident proves," he pointed out. "And I was behaving responsibly! Just imagine the danger if the time machine were to fall into the wrong hands!"

That was funny. Doc could have sworn he heard

that triple sonic boom—the same kind of boom that resulted from using the time machine. Oh, well. There were a lot of things in 2015 capable of making that kind of noise. He shifted some of Jennifer's weight into Marty's arms.

"My only regret," Doc added, almost as an afterthought, "is that I'll never get a chance to visit my favorite historical era—the old west. But time traveling is just too dangerous. Better I devote myself to studying the other great mystery of the universe—women."

Marty shook his head.

"Doc, if you can solve that one, let me know."

With Jennifer between them, they walked back to the DeLorean.

Marty climbed into the passenger seat, and he and Doc managed to lower Jennifer onto Marty's lap. Einstein jumped into the back as Doc got behind the wheel. The scientist quickly entered their destination data. They were going home—to 1985!

"We'll come back after dark," Doc explained, setting their arrival for the middle of the night. "The less we're seen, the better."

Doc turned around. The dog was playing with something in the backseat.

"Einie, get that junk out of your mouth!"

Doc pulled the crumpled silver bag from between Einstein's teeth.

A silver bag? Something tugged at the back of Doc's mind. Where had he seen a silver bag before. Where did that dog find this stuff, anyway?

Doc started the time machine. It was time to go

back where they belonged, where they could stop worrying and just let time take care of itself.

Marty kept a firm grip on the unconscious Jennifer. He wanted to keep anything more from happening to her on the way home.

"Altitude, seven-thousand feet," Doc announced. "That should be high enough." He glanced around to check on his passengers. "Marty, Einie, brace yourselves for temporal displacement!"

Doc floored the accelerator, straight for a row of floating lane markers.

They reached eighty-eight miles per hour in a matter of seconds.

There was a blinding flash of light from the flux capacitor, accompanied by that moment when you seemed to go from traveling at eighty-eight miles per hour, to not traveling at all—as if, for an instant, you were suspended outside of time and space. Then there were the three sonic booms, and you were going eighty-eight miles per hour again—except you were sometime else.

Marty looked out the window. Wherever they were, the floating lane markers were gone. It was night, and all he could see were tiny lights far below.

"Did we make it?" Marty asked.

As if in answer, a 747 jumbo jet roared much too close overhead. The DeLorean shook violently for a moment before Doc stabilized it again.

"We're back," Doc agreed. "Now let's get Jennifer home."

He took the DeLorean down slowly, searching the lights below for familiar streets.

A moment later, he set the car down on a quiet road outside of town as the wheels slipped back into place underneath.

They drove the rest of the way to Jennifer's house. Even in the dark, Marty could see THE PARKERS in big block letters on their mailbox.

Marty and Doc managed to get Jennifer out of the car, and gently carried her toward the house. Doc nodded ahead to the front porch.

"Let's put her in the swing."

Wouldn't that just confuse Jennifer more when she woke up?

"But she left from my house," Marty pointed out.

Doc thought about that for a second.

"True," he replied reasonably, "but when she revives here at her own house, and it's dark, the disorientation will help convince her that it was all a dream."

Hmm, Marty thought. That sounded logical enough.

"Okay," Marty agreed, "you're the doc."

They set her down on the porch swing. Jennifer began to snore softly. Marty guessed everything was going to be all right. But why did he still feel uneasy? Maybe it had something to do with the time traveling—sort of like jet lag.

Still, there was something different. He turned away from Jennifer, ready to follow Doc back down to the car—but stopped when he saw the heavy iron grillwork that covered the windows to either side of the front door.

"I must be crazy," he muttered, half to himself. "I don't remember bars on these windows." Maybe, he thought, that time-lag business played tricks with your memory, too.

"Oh well, I guess—" He had to get himself back together. He paused to take a deep breath, but stopped almost as soon as he started to inhale.

"Jeez, something really stinks!" He barely kept himself from coughing. It was really foul!

Doc sniffed the air and made a face of his own. "Must be a fire somewhere. We'd better get going."

Marty glanced over his shoulder at the sleeping Jennifer.

Doc reassured Marty as they hurried back to the car. "She'll be fine. I'll take you home. You can change clothes and come back for her in your truck."

Marty guessed that made sense, too. He shrugged and followed the older man.

"You're the doc."

They got back in the DeLorean and headed for Marty's home, over in the Lyon Estates.

Marty still couldn't shake the feeling that things weren't quite right. It probably had something to do with coming back here from the future—a future he realized he didn't know too much about.

Maybe that's what was bothering him—getting a glimpse of the future, but not *his* future, or his family's. Heaven knew it looked different to him around here—back in 1985, in what should be familiar surroundings. He noticed a boarded-up window here and there as they drove through the late-night streets, and there seemed to be twice as much trash everywhere as he had ever seen before. Even the road was awful. Didn't Hill Valley ever fill in their potholes?

But the more he thought about it, the more he guessed time travel had something to do with all of this, not only this trip to the future, but his earlier visit to the past. He was probably "gaining a sense of perspective"—that was the sort of thing his parents would say—and seeing things about Hill Valley he never would have noticed before.

Or maybe he was just tired and grumpy from all that action in the future.

Doc pulled the DeLorean past the lion gates and into Marty's neighborhood. They stopped in front of Marty's house. Marty jumped out and waved good night.

"If you need me," Doc called out, patting the steering wheel, "I'll be back at my lab, dismantling this thing. Let me know if you have any trouble convincing her it was all a dream."

"Or a nightmare," Marty added as he started up the walk.

Doc nodded sagely, then drove away.

Marty stopped, halfway up to the house.

He heard a couple sounds in the distance, explosions, really, like a car backfiring over and over again. It almost sounded like gunfire.

In Hill Valley? Get serious, McFly!

Marty hurried to the front door, anyway. He stuck his key in the lock. It wouldn't turn. Marty jiggled the key. It still didn't work.

"What the hell?" Marty whispered.

Somebody had changed the lock. But why? He supposed it must have something to do with the stuff he had done back in 1955, and the changes that stuff had caused—like his father becoming a successful writer and all—here in 1985. But, if that was true, shouldn't Marty's key have changed to fit the new lock? That's the way he thought this time travel stuff worked. He guessed he still really didn't understand Doc's explanations, after all.

Oh, well. It was too late to try to figure out the mysteries of science. If he couldn't get in the front door, he'd go around the back way. He would have another chance to figure out everything in the morning.

The gate leading into the backyard was locked, too, with an impressive looking padlock. This wasn't going to be as easy as he thought. But there was more than one way to get into his bedroom.

He climbed on top of a garbage can, then jumped over the gate. There! That wasn't so hard. He walked a few more paces until he was opposite his bedroom, and tried one of the windows. It opened easily. That was a relief! Marty had started to think there might be something wrong here.

He climbed quickly inside, easing his foot down so that it would hit the top of his dresser.

Wait a minute! The dresser wasn't there!

Marty lost his balance and fell into the room. Onto a bed.

Somebody screamed in his ear.

• Chapter
Ten •

The light went on. A young black girl, maybe eleven or twelve, stared at him from less than a foot away, clutching her covers up to her neck.

"Momma!" she shrieked. "Dad! Help!"

"Hey," Marty demanded, "who are you? What are you—" He hesitated, looking around. "—doing—in my—room?"

This place had changed. His model airplanes, mini-amplifier, and posters of sports stars were gone, replaced by pink wallpaper, stuffed animals, and posters of Michael Jackson.

Marty didn't recognize this place at all. This wasn't his room.

This was a girl's room.

"Help! Daddy! Help!" the room's rightful owner screamed as she jumped from bed. She grabbed a handful of things from her bureau and started to throw them at Marty.

Marty ducked. This *should* have been his room. Where had he gone wrong?

The door slammed open, and the rest of the family rushed in, father, mother, and younger brother. All three stared at Marty.

Marty was not pleased to see that the father was carrying a baseball bat.

"Freeze, sucker!" the father announced as he raised the bat above his head.

Marty raised his hands.

"Okay, take it easy," he said slowly and clearly. "I don't want any trouble."

That didn't seem to impress the father at all. He raised his bat even higher.

"Well, you got trouble now, you no good trash! What are you doing in here with my daughter?"

Marty looked around the room, as if an explanation might be hiding somewhere.

"Nothing!" he insisted hastily. "It's all a mistake! I'm in the wrong house!"

The younger brother jumped up and down. He was really getting into this.

"Whoop him, Dad!" he yelled happily. "He's lying!"

"Shut up, Harold," his father told him. He looked past Marty at his daughter. "Loretta, did he touch you?"

The girl nodded her head vigorously.

"He jumped on me!"

He did not, Marty thought! He more like—fell on her. But how could he explain that?

The father took another step into the room.

"Please, I'm sorry!" Marty yelled back. "I just made a mistake!"

"Damn right you made a mistake!"

The father swung the baseball bat. Marty jumped aside. The bat smashed into one of the girl's bookshelves.

"Dad, stop!" Loretta screamed. "You're breaking my stuff!"

But her father was beyond listening. He swung again, missing Marty but smashing half the bottles on the top of the girl's dresser. Loretta ran across the room and started to beat on her father.

This was Marty's chance. He had to get out of here! He jumped over Harold, past father, daughter, and mother, and ran from the room.

Whatever had happened, at least this house was laid out the same way as the one he remembered, and he easily made it down the hall to the front door. He unlocked the door and ran out into the street.

He stopped to take one final look back at the place. It sure looked like his house.

The father ran out onto the porch, bat still in hand. Marty decided it was time to leave the neighborhood.

"That's right," the father yelled as the rest of his family came out to join him, "you keep running, sucker! And you tell that white trash realty company that I ain't selling, you hear? We ain't gonna be forced out!"

"Lewis," the mother lectured her husband, "tomorrow you're going to put bars on all the windows, understand?"

"Like hell, I will," the father replied, shouting more at Marty than at his family. "I won't have my family livin' in a jail! I won't have that!"

Marty heard more explosions in the distance. Boy, those sure sounded like gunfire!

But the father wasn't following him. After he had run a couple blocks, Marty slowed down to catch his breath and figure out just where he was.

A police car raced around the corner, sirens blaring, flashers blazing. Marty barely had time to jump out of the way before the cops sped by.

What was going on here?

He saw something bright across a yard a few hundred feet in front of him. He walked toward it, and realized it was the broad yellow tape cops used to keep crowds from walking all over the evidence. DO NOT CROSS—POLICE INVESTIGATION IN PROGRESS. Marty stopped just before the tape, and saw two chalk outlines on the pavement on the other side—outlines in the shape of people. Inside each outline were darker spots that glistened in the streetlights. Marty realized those spots must be blood.

This couldn't be his old neighborhood. Sure, he recognized houses, and the street signs were right, but still . . .

"This is nuts," he said aloud. But he kept on walking. What else could he do?

It was even worse when he got to the corner. There, in front of him, was Hill Valley High School, or—maybe he should say—what was left of Hill Valley High School. The place looked like it had been fire-bombed. Only half of it was still standing, and that was covered with deep black soot. What windows were left were boarded over, and the whole place was surrounded by a barbed wire fence—as if the building had been in the middle of some kind of a war zone.

But, even in ruins, the place was definitely the high school. So Doc had brought him back to the right place. This was Hill Valley, all right.

That meant something else had gone wrong.

"It's got to be the wrong year!" Marty said aloud.

He walked slowly across the street. Something must have gone wrong with Doc's time machine. But where—or when—had the time machine left him?

There was a newspaper on the porch in front of him. That would tell him what he needed to know. He ran onto the porch and scooped up the folded paper. He opened it, looking for the dateline under the masthead.

Saturday, October 26, 1985.

"1985!" Marty yelled. "It can't be!"

There was a sound right behind him—like somebody pumping a shotgun. Marty felt something cold and hard pressed against the side of his head—something like the barrel of a shotgun.

A voice spoke behind him.

"So you're the son of a bitch who's been stealing my newspapers!"

Marty knew that voice, sure to strike terror into the hearts of teenagers throughout Hill Valley. He turned, slowly and carefully.

"Mr. Strickland!"

The bald vice-principal in charge of discipline tipped his gun down slightly and frowned back at Marty. He looked even more fierce than the teenager remembered. Maybe it was because Mr. Strickland had somehow gotten a long and livid knife scar across his face that made him look like he was going to kill Marty at any minute. Or maybe it was that flak jacket Mr. Strickland was wearing over his bathrobe. Whatever it was, he looked twice as mean as he ever had before.

But Strickland still hadn't recognized him.

"It's me, sir!" He pointed at his chest. "Marty! Marty McFly!"

"Who?" Strickland demanded.

"Marty McFly. Don't you know me, sir?" What sort of world would this be if the vice-principal in charge of detention didn't recognize him?

Strickland lowered his gun, squinting at Marty in the darkness.

"I've never seen you before," he said with a shake of his head. "But you look like a slacker!"

Wait a minute! Maybe Strickland recognized him after all!

"That's right!" Marty exclaimed enthusiastically. "You're always calling me a slacker! I'm always late; you're always giving me tardy slips."

Strickland still stared as if he had never seen this teenager before. There had to be some way to remind him. Of course!

"You just gave me detention last week!" Marty added happily.

Strickland nodded to himself, as if Marty had confirmed something he had known all along.

"Last week?" the vice-principal snapped. "Now I know you're lying." He nodded across the street. "The school's been burned down for six years."

Strickland glanced meaningfully at the shotgun.

"Now you've got exactly three seconds to get off my porch with your nuts intact."

He curled his finger around the trigger.

"One."

What? He was going to shoot Marty? But he couldn't!

"Mr. Strickland!" Marty insisted. "You've got to tell me what's going on here!"

"Two," was Strickland's only reply. He raised the shotgun.

A car screeched up to the curb, full of scruffy teens sporting leather jackets and multicolored mohawks. And, Marty noticed, all of them had guns, too.

"Eat lead, Strickland!" the mangiest of the bunch

announced. The entire punk-filled carload opened fire. Bullets strafed the porch. Strickland ducked for cover, as Marty vaulted over the railing. He was in the middle of a war!

Strickland came back up shooting.

"Eat buckshot, slackers!"

Marty ran like hell. He had to get out of here!

But where was he?

And where could he go?

•Chapter Eleven•

Marty ran all the way to Courthouse Square. He had to go this way to get to Doc's lab, anyway—if Doc's lab was still there, and if Marty could make it that far without getting shot. In the meantime, maybe he could find somebody here to tell him what was going on.

He walked past the HILL VALLEY—A NICE PLACE TO LIVE sign. It was riddled with bullet holes.

The Courthouse had changed, too. Someone had turned it into a hotel—and what a hotel! It looked like something straight out of Las Vegas, full of neon and glaring lights. Marty couldn't believe it when he read the sign:

Biff Tannen? Marty thought. *The* Biff Tannen?

But there was more to the sign, below the name, flashing one after another:

> HOTEL
>> RESORT
>>> CASINO
>>>> GIRLS

And that wasn't all! Right in the middle of the sign was a huge portrait of Biff, lighting a cigar with a hundred-dollar bill.

It was bright! It was garish! It had absolutely no taste! It *had* to be the same Biff Tannen!

Marty was overwhelmed. It was the middle of the night, and the place was doing a fantastic business! People streamed in and out of the door marked CA-SINO. Most of the customers were fat, middle-aged men in business suits, each with a much younger woman—sometimes two—on one or both of his arms, and all of them talking and laughing.

Whatever they were saying, though, was completely lost in the roar of motorcycles. The grass and hedges of the square were gone, paved over with asphalt, and filled now with a hundred bikers, drag racing and revving their engines.

As Marty looked around, he realized the whole square was different. The aerobics place and family stores had disappeared, replaced by adult book stores, bars, pawn shops, bail bondsmen, and porno theaters—and all of those were open for business, too. The whole town seemed to be open all night!

And behind it all, on every side of the square, even towering over the Pleasure Paradise, were row after row of tall industrial smokestacks, all spewing thick smoke into the darkness.

Hill Valley certainly had changed.

The front door of the Biff Tannen Pleasure Paradise slammed open, and three men emerged, half-dragging, half-carrying a fourth. It looked like three bouncers getting rid of a drunk. At least, Marty reflected, that sort of thing hadn't changed.

Marty could have sworn he knew those bouncers.

They were older than the last time he had seen them, but those three bouncers looked an awful lot like those guys that used to hang around with Biff back in the fifties—Match, Skinhead and 3-D. All of them wore suits now. Match now wore a cowboy hat, while Skinhead's crew cut was a lot grayer than before. And 3-D's glasses were a lot fancier. The way they gleamed under the neon, they almost looked like they had jewels embedded in the rims. But all three were the same bullies they'd been back in 1955.

"And don't ever come beggin' for drinks in here again!" 3-D yelled. "Friggin' lush!"

The drunk picked himself up off the pavement.

"Hey," he called after the bouncers, his voice slightly slurred, "can't you guys take a joke?" The drunk reached into the pocket of his ragged coat and fished out a pint bottle, which he drained in a single gulp. He threw the empty bottle in the general direction of the hotel, then started to stagger down the street.

There was something disturbingly familiar about that drunk—the curly hair and crooked smile, the way he laughed, even the way he staggered. In fact, the drunk looked just like Marty's older brother!

Marty walked quickly—but very cautiously—through the bikers that filled the asphalt-covered Courthouse Square, past roaring fires in oil drums and seven-foot-tall guys swinging chains, toward the Pleasure Paradise.

"Dave!" Marty called.

The drunk turned unsteadily to look at him.

"Marty!" he called, his unfocused face breaking into a broad grin. He gave his brother an exaggerated wave. "Hey, bro, what's happening!" He frowned as Marty got closer. "Hey, you're looking kind of ragged there. What, did you sleep in your clothes again last night?"

His brother should talk, Marty thought. He had hardly ever seen anyone look so down and out. But now, maybe, he could get some answers.

"Dave, my God, what's happened to you? What's happened to the town? What's going on around here?"

"Oh, all this?" Dave waved generously at the drag racers on the street. "It's the biker's convention!"

Dave turned slowly back to his brother. It seemed to take his eyes a moment to focus.

"So, Marty," he said at last, "when'd you get back?"

Marty had no idea what Dave was talking about. "Back?" he asked. "Back from where?"

"Well," Dave drawled in response, "if you don't know, how do you expect me to tell you?"

He laughed as if that was the funniest thing he had ever heard.

Dave grabbed his brother's arm. "Hey, let's go have a few, huh? You got money, don't you?" He started to pull Marty toward the tavern.

Marty pulled back.

"What are you talking about, Dave? I'm under age!"

His brother stopped and stared at him.

"Under age? Quit kiddin' around! You been over fourteen since—" He paused with a frown, trying to concentrate. "Since—" He shrugged and grinned, as if concentration was far beyond someone in his state. "Well, since your fourteenth birthday!"

Dave thought that remark was funnier than the last one. He roared and roared.

"Fourteen?" Marty asked. Did his brother mean the drinking age around here was fourteen? Oh, well, it didn't matter. There was only one thing that did: What had happened to everybody?

"Listen Dave, I gotta find Mom and Dad."

Dave stared back at his brother, suddenly sober.

"Dad? You gotta find Dad? That's sick, Marty. That's really sick. What's the matter with you, anyway?" He shook his head, as if he couldn't believe anyone could be that unfeeling. "And since when are you and Mom on speaking terms again?"

Marty was getting more confused with every passing minute here.

"Speaking terms?" he asked. What was going on here? But, maybe, Marty thought, any explanation Dave might give him would confuse him even more.

"Look, do you know where she is?" he asked Dave instead. "Can you tell me where I can find Mom?"

Dave shrugged as if he could care less.

"Same place as usual, I guess. In there."

He pointed toward Biff Tannen's Pleasure Paradise.

In there?

Marty turned back to his brother, but Dave had already staggered halfway back toward the bar. Maybe, Marty thought, he should stop Dave. But he needed to find his mother, and figure out what had happened.

He walked toward the hotel.

Just before the hotel entrance was the door to another building, the BIFF TANNEN MUSEUM, according to the neon sign out front. Marty stopped for a second to stare at the display area in front of the ticket window.

There, in the middle of the display, was the black roadster Biff had driven back in 1955—the same one that had gotten bashed in in that collision with a manure truck. Except now the car had been totally restored; it was so sleek and brightly polished that it almost looked brand new. And next to that was a

lifelike wax figure of Biff! It was a pretty good like-
ness, too—the same burly body and sloping forehead. They had even gotten the smirk right.

A deep voice was speaking over a loudspeaker
somewhere nearby.

"Of course, we've all heard the legend. But who
is *the man*? Inside, you will learn how Biff Tannen
became one of the richest and most powerful men
in America!"

Biff Tannen was one of the richest and most powerful men in America? That would explain a lot.
There was a video monitor over at the other end of
the display. Marty walked over to get a closer look.
The monitor was showing a photo montage in color
and black-and-white—pictures from Biff's childhood, his high school sports triumphs, shots of the
exhibits inside. The same, deep announcer's voice
spoke in the background.

"Learn the amazing history of the Tannen family,
starting with the grandfather, Buford 'Mad Dog'
Tannen, fastest gun in the west."

An old, brown tintype appeared on the screen,
showing a western gunfighter who looked just like
Biff!

"See Biff's humble beginnings—" the announcer
continued proudly. There were more childhood photos. "And how a trip to the racetrack on his twenty-
first birthday made him a millionaire overnight."

On the screen a photo flashed of Biff jumping in
the air, wads of money clutched in both fists. The
announcer went on. "Share the excitement of a fab-

ulous winning streak that earned him the nickname, 'The Luckiest Man on Earth!' ''

Marty glanced over at the woman in the ticket booth. She was staring at him. Did he know her from somewhere? She picked up the phone and started talking into it.

Marty turned back to the video monitor.

"Learn how Biff parlayed that lucky winning streak into the vast empire called 'BiffCo'!"

There was a photo of BiffCo Corporate headquarters, followed by a shot of row after row of smokestacks—those same smokestacks Marty saw all over town!

"Witness how Biff changed the face of Hill Valley, making it a center of industrial growth. Discover how, in 1969, Biff successfully lobbied to legalize gambling throughout the land—"

There were shots of spinning roulette wheels, cards being dealt, and happy, smiling faces.

"—to put the dream he had realized into the reach of all Americans. Marvel at Biff's ongoing relationships with the rich and famous."

There were a bunch of shots of Biff with celebrities, prominent politicians, and talk-show hosts.

"Meet the women who shared in his passion as he searched for true love."

More photos followed—top models, starlets, women in swimsuits on magazine covers.

"And relive Biff's happiest moment as—in 1973— he realized his lifelong dream by marrying his high school sweetheart, Lorraine Baines McFly."

Lorraine Baines McFly? The monitor showed a home movie of Biff coming out of a church with Marty's mother!

Biff grinned into the camera. "Third time's the charm." He turned, and kissed Marty's mother full on the mouth.

"No!" Marty screamed. He must be dreaming! Anything but this! *"No!"*

There was a hand on his shoulder.

Marty turned. There were three guys standing behind him—three guys he knew.

It was Match, 3-D, and Skinhead.

"Hold on there, squirt," Skinhead said with a sneer. "You're comin' with us. Upstairs."

Marty tried to pull away.

"Let me go, dammit!" he yelled.

Match stuck his index finger in Marty's face. "Look, we can do this the easy way—or the hard way."

Marty wasn't going anywhere with these thugs. 3-D pulled a blackjack out of his pocket. Marty pulled back from Skinhead's grip. He had to get out of here!

3-D chuckled as he swung the blackjack down in an arc toward Marty's skull.

"The easy way," 3-D said.

Those were the last words Marty heard.

•Chapter
Twelve•

Marty felt something cold pressed to his forehead. He groaned and opened his eyes. It was dark in here, the only light coming from a picture window that looked out on a dull gray sky.

He was lying on a bed, and he could see the outline of a woman standing next to him. Even in the dim light, he thought he recognized her.

"Mom?" he called softly. "Is that you?"

Cool fingers patted the back of his palm.

"Shh," his mother replied. "Just relax, Marty. You've been asleep for almost two hours."

Asleep? He had been asleep?

"Ohh," he moaned, "what a horrible nightmare— it was terrible."

"Well," his mother replied gently, "you're safe and sound now."

She was right, too. Marty felt really relaxed for the first time since—well, since before he'd ever seen Doc Brown's time machine. He could feel his eyes sliding closed.

"Back home," his mother continued cheerily, "on the good old twenty-seventh floor."

Marty's eyes snapped opened.

Twenty-seventh floor?

Marty sat up. This wasn't home. Even in the semidarkness he could see he was in a big room cluttered with stuff—a room he'd never seen before. And the bed was round. Everything had changed.

The nightmare wasn't over.

It got worse when his mother sat down next to the bed and turned on the light.

His mother had changed, too.

Marty didn't know what was more shocking—the curly wig; the heavy makeup and false eyelashes; the enormous earrings, necklace, bracelets and rings, all glittering with diamonds; or the spangled, low-cut evening gown. Boy, his mother had changed! The way she was done up now, she looked like some barmaid, or the wife of some evangelist he'd seen on TV.

Actually, one change was most dramatic. It embarrassed him to even notice it—his own mother! She seemed to have had some surgery done to the upper area of—especially in that tight dress, her torso was—well, there was no other way to put it: Her cleavage was certainly ample.

She was staring at him as if she expected him to say something.

"Mom!" he managed at last. "You're so—so—uh—*big!*"

Marty frowned. That wasn't what he wanted to say. But what *could* he say?

His mother smiled at him reassuringly, as if her son could never say anything wrong. She opened a cigarette case encrusted with diamonds, then picked up a cigarette between two deep red, sculpted nails, and fitted it into a diamond-inlaid cigarette holder. Placing the mouthpiece of the holder between her deep red lips, she lit the cigarette with a solid gold lighter, and inhaled as if the smoke was the breath of life.

She looked over at her son again.

"Everything's going to be fine, Marty." She raised one overplucked eyebrow. "Are you hungry? We can call room service—"

Marty swung his legs off the bed. This whole room was as overdecorated as his mother. The wallpaper was inlaid with golden thread. The paintings were set in heavy wooden frames painted in gold leaf. Golden tinted chandeliers hung from the ceiling.

He looked out the window, past the gold-braided drapes. There, twenty-seven floors below, he could see the twinkling lights of Hill Valley, and, beyond that, the ring of factories, with a hundred smokestacks belching forth thick, black smoke that blotted out the stars. He must be on the very top floor of Biff Tannen's Pleasure Paradise.

But why was the Paradise here? How did a place like this end up in Hill Valley, run by Biff Tannen, of all people? A nice place like Hill Valley ending up like this. Marty felt a coldness deep inside, like an ice cube in the pit of his stomach. Marty couldn't think of anything to say.

"I forgot," his mother jumped in, filling the void left by his silence. She waved happily at their surroundings with her manicured nails. "You haven't seen the penthouse since we redecorated!"

We? Marty thought. Did that mean his whole family lived there? But what was his family doing, living in the penthouse of the Paradise?

"Lorraine?" a gruff voice called from the other side of the closed bedroom door. "Where are you?"

Marty's mother frowned.

"It's your father."

She took another quick drag on her cigarette.

"My father?" Marty asked. That gruff voice didn't sound anything like George McFly.

Somebody kicked open the bedroom door.

Biff Tannen walked in. He had changed, too. He was in better shape than the last time Marty had seen him—in 1985, that is. His clothes were fancier, too—a silk suit of pastel green, and a shirt open halfway down his chest to show off a dozen gold chains.

His three old gang buddies followed him into the

room. All three of them smirked at Marty, as if they had been taking lessons from their boss.

Marty stared. His father? This was what his mother meant? Biff Tannen?

"My *father*?" Marty yelled.

Biff glared at Marty as if the teenager had just crawled out from under a rock.

"You're supposed to be in Switzerland," he snapped, "you little son of a bitch!! Did you get kicked out of *another* boarding school?" He waggled a pudgy index finger at Marty's mother. "Damn it, Lorraine! Do you know how much perfectly good dough I've blown on this no-good kid of yours? On all three of them?"

Mom took a couple of quick, nervous puffs from her cigarette before she replied.

"What the hell do you care?" she retorted. "We can afford it! The least we can do is make a better life for our children!"

She walked over to a portable bar next to the picture window, and poured herself three fingers of scotch. She drained her glass without taking a breath.

Biff pointed his shaking finger at Marty now.

"Marty's *your* kid, not mine, and all the money in the world wouldn't do jack shit for that lazy bum! He's a butthead, just like his old man was!"

Marty's mother slammed her glass down. "Don't you dare speak that way about George! You're not even half the man he was!"

Biff took two quick steps across the room and slapped her full across the face.

"Never talk to me like that, you hear me?" Biff growled, his hand lifted to hit her again. "Ever!"

Marty's mother cringed.

This was too much! Marty couldn't stand here and watch this happen. He ran for Biff.

3-D and Skinhead grabbed him and pulled him away.

Marty's mother rubbed her cheek and jaw. Even with the heavy makeup, Marty could see an angry red welt forming there.

Biff smirked at the captive Marty.

"Always the little hothead, huh?" He walked up to Marty. "Come on, want to take a poke at me?"

It would be a little tough, Marty thought, to take a poke at Biff while his goons were still holding onto him.

Biff sucker-punched Marty in the stomach.

"Damn it, Biff!" she hollered. "That's it. I'm leaving!" She turned and walked purposefully toward the door.

"Sure, walk out!" Biff called after her. "And I'll cut you off—you and your kids!"

She paused in the doorway.

"I can get Dave's probation revoked, and he'll have to go to prison." Biff's smirk spread across his face. He was really enjoying this. "Maybe he'll even end up sharing a cell with your brother Joey. And Linda—I'll close her accounts and she can settle her debts with the bank all by herself. And Marty, well—"

"Okay, Biff," she murmured. "You win. I'll—" It took her a moment to get the final word out. "—stay."

Mom's shoulders slumped in defeat. She turned around and walked slowly back to the bar.

Biff grinned, showing all his teeth.

"Damn right you'll stay." He turned to Marty, the smile gone. "As for you, I'll be back up here in an hour." He looked down at his fingers as his right hand curled into a fist. "So you'd better *not* be—"

Biff stormed from the room. His thugs let Marty go and followed their boss.

Marty looked over at his mother. She looked away, as if she couldn't face the questions in his gaze.

"I had it coming, Marty," she said slowly. "I was wrong. He was right."

Marty couldn't believe this.

"Mom, what are you saying? You're actually defending him!"

She shook her head. "He's my husband, and he takes care of all of us, and he deserves our respect."

This got worse with everything she said.

"Your husband?" Marty yelled. He was getting really upset. "Respect? How can he be your husband? How could you leave Dad for him?"

Mom looked back to Marty, the pain in her eyes turned to concern.

"Leave Dad?" she asked gently. "Marty are you feeling all right?"

"No!" Marty replied vehemently. "I'm *not* feeling all right! I don't understand one damned thing that's going on around here and why nobody can give me a simple straight answer!"

His mother's brow furrowed as she shook her head again.

"They must have really hit you over the head hard."

But Marty had had enough of this nonsense. He needed some answers!

"Mom," he insisted, "I want just one thing. Where's my father? Where's George McFly?"

His mother reached out her hand to almost, but not quite, touch her son.

"Marty," she said, slowly and sadly. "George— your father—is in the same place he's been for the last twelve years. Oak Park Cemetery."

Marty ran.

He raced across the cemetery in the bright moonlight, darting wildly from row to row of gravestones, barely avoiding dead trees and marble monuments in his panicked scramble to know the truth. He scanned the names etched in granite as he ran, half of him searching for the gravestone with his father's name, the other half still somehow hoping, wishing, praying that his mother had lied, that there would be no gravestone, that his father would still be alive.

He stopped, and took a step backward.

There it was. A simple, granite marker, smaller than most of the others round it, with three lines etched in the stone:

IN LOVING MEMORY
GEORGE DOUGLAS MCFLY
April 1, 1938–March 15, 1973

"1973!" Marty shouted to the sky. "No!" He fell to his knees in front of the stone. "Please, God, no! This can't be happening!"

A shadow fell across the gravestone. Marty looked up. There was someone standing behind him.

"I'm afraid it *is* happening, Marty," a familiar voice said. "All of it."

"Doc!" Marty cried as he turned.

Doc Brown nodded soberly down at Marty.

"When I learned about your father," he explained, "I figured you'd come here."

Marty stood so quickly that he almost lost his balance.

"Then you know what happened to him?" he asked. "You know what happened on—" He turned back to the gravestone to check the date. "March 15, 1973?"

Doc nodded again.

"Yes, Marty, I know."

Doc led the way into his lab—or at least what was left of it.

The place had been trashed. A lot of Doc's gizmos

had been torn apart. Pieces of experiments and bits of broken glass littered the floor, crunching underfoot as they walked. The windows had all been smashed, and most of them had been boarded up. The electricity was gone, too. Doc had lit a pair of candles when they entered, and handed one to Marty. He then proceeded to walk around the edges of the lab, lighting other strategically placed candles from the first one's flame until the entire room was filled with a warm glow.

It didn't matter, though. It could have stayed dark for all Marty cared. His father—dead?

Doc waved Marty over to the one table left standing, and the large and heavy bound volume open there. As Marty brought his candle close to the pages, he realized this was one of those bound collections of newspapers—the kind you sometimes found in libraries.

The book was open to the local Hill Valley paper, dated March 16, 1973, the day after his father died.

Marty stared at the headline:

GEORGE MCFLY MURDERED!

And, in smaller type below:

Author Shot Dead in Apparent Holdup
Enroute to Receive Book Award!
Police Baffled, Search for Witnesses!

"I went to the public library to try to make some sense out of all of the madness," Doc explained over

Marty's shoulder. "The place was boarded up—shut down. So I broke in and—" He waved at the book and a couple more like it still on the floor—"Borrowed some newspapers."

Marty glanced up from his reading.

"But Doc, how can all this be happening? I mean, it's like we're in hell or something."

Doc looked between the boards, studying the world beyond one of the broken windows.

"No, it's Hill Valley," he replied curtly, "although I can't imagine hell being much worse."

Einstein whined by Doc's feet. Doc glanced down.

"I know, Einie," he said with a sigh. "The lab's an awful mess." He pulled a cushion out of the rubble and dusted it off, then placed it on the floor. Einstein dutifully sat on it.

Doc turned back to Marty.

"You see, Marty," Doc explained in his best lecture mode, "the continuum has been disrupted, creating a new temporal event sequence resulting in this alternate reality—alternate to us, but reality for everyone else."

Marty shook his head. He couldn't understand a word.

"English, Doc," he requested.

Doc picked up a fallen blackboard and propped it up against the table. Another moment's search, and he had located a piece of chalk.

Doc drew a straight line on the blackboard.

"Imagine that this line represents time. Here's the present, 1985—"

He wrote "1985" in the center of the line.

"The past—"

He wrote "PAST" to the left.

"And the future."

To the right of "1985", he scrawled a big, fat "F."

"Now, prior to this point in time—" He pointed again to 1985. "Somewhere in the past—" he put an "x" above the line in the past, "the time line was skewed." He drew another line, from the middle of the past, straight down toward the bottom of the blackboard. "Resulting in this alternate 1985. Alternate to you, me, and Einstein, but reality for everyone else."

Marty shook his head. "I still don't get it, Doc."

Doc reached in the pocket of his lab coat and pulled out a silver bag.

"Recognize this?" he asked. He handed the bag to Marty. "It's the bag the sports book came in. I know, because the receipt was still inside." Doc passed the receipt over, too. Yep, there it was, the name of the antique store, followed by the words: "PURCHASED: GREY'S SPORTS ALMANAC 1950–2000" and the incredibly inflated price. It was the book Marty had bought, and here was the bag he had carried it in. But Doc had thrown the book and the bag away, hadn't he?

"I found them in the time machine," Doc continued, "along with this—"

Doc pulled out a brass ornament on the top of a broken pole. Marty had seen that ornament before. It was in the shape of a fist. In fact, he had personally felt that ornament, when a certain older gentleman had knocked him with it and called Marty a butthead—in 2015! So Marty wasn't at all surprised when he read the name engraved on the palm: Biff H. Tannen.

"This was the top of Biff's cane," Marty explained, although he guessed that Doc already knew it. "Old Biff, in the future. And you found it *in* the DeLorean?"

"Correct!" Doc raised a finger to drive home his point. "It was in the time machine because Biff was in the time machine, *with the sports almanac*!"

"Holy shit!" Marty replied.

"You see," Doc continued, obviously proud of his deductive abilities, "while we were in the future—" he pointed at the big "F" on the blackboard—"Biff got the sports book, stole the time machine, went back in time, and gave the book to himself at some point here—" he drew a long arc, all the way from the "F" to the "X"— "in the past!"

He picked up another of those large newspaper volumes from the floor and opened the book to the place he had marked with a piece of broken ceiling tile.

"Look."

The headline on this issue read:

HV MAN WINS BIG AT RACES!

Underneath that was a photo of Biff collecting his winnings at the pay window.

Doc slapped the paper in front of Marty.

"It says right here that Biff made his first million betting on a horse race in 1958. He wasn't just lucky. He *knew*—because he had all the race results in the sports almanac!" Doc's point-making finger rose one more time. "That's how he made his entire fortune!"

He pulled one more thing out of his lab coat pocket.

"Look at his pocket with the magnifying glass," he told Marty.

Marty took the handle of the glass from Doc and held the lens over the photo. There, sticking out of Biff's pocket, was the top half of the sports almanac!

"That bastard stole my idea!" He put down the glass and looked up at his scientist friend. "Doc, he must have overhead me when I told you about—"

He stopped himself midsentence. This sports almanac scheme had been his idea. He was to blame for everything that happened to Hill Valley!

"This whole thing's my fault," he said aloud, his voice little more than a whisper. "If I hadn't bought that book, none of this would have happened."

Doc waved both his hands, as if Marty's fears were groundless.

"Well, that's all in the past," Doc reassured him.

"You mean in the future," Marty corrected him.

"Whatever," Doc replied, "it demonstrates precisely how time travel can be misused and why the time machine must be destroyed—" he paused to swallow—"after we straighten all of this out."

"Right!" Marty agreed. So maybe there was a way out of this, after all. "We've got to go back to the future and stop Biff from ever stealing the time machine!"

Doc shook his head with a frown. "We can't, because if we travel into the future from *this* point in time—" he pointed to the line going to the bottom of the blackboard—"it would be the future of this reality, in which Biff is wealthy and married to your mother, and in which *this* has happened to me!"

Doc picked up a third book, and turned to another page marked by a smaller piece of ceiling tile. He pushed the book back in front of Marty.

The newspaper was dated July, 1983. The headline at the top of the page read:

EMMETT BROWN COMMITTED.
Crackpot Inventor Declared Legally Insane!

Below the headlines was a picture of Doc, in a straitjacket! And next to that was another headline:

NIXON TO SEEK 5TH TERM
Vows to End Vietnam War by 1985!

This was terrible! The whole world had changed.

"No, Marty," Doc went on, "our only chance to repair the present is in the past, at the point where the time line skewed into this tangent." Doc slapped his fist into his open palm. "Somehow, we must find out the specific circumstances of how, where, and when young Biff got his hands on that sports almanac!"

They had to find out something from Biff? How could they possibly do that?

Marty glanced at the twin headlines in front of him; his father dead, Doc Brown committed to an asylum. Marty ripped the page about his father's death out of the book and stuffed it inside his jacket. Something had to be done, and he realized there was only one person who could do it.

Marty had gotten them into this. Now he'd have to get them out. It was up to him to confront Biff and get the truth.

"I'll ask him," was all Marty said.

•Chapter
Thirteen•

"The heart, Ramone," Clint said. "Don't forget the heart."

Ramone fired.

It had been surprisingly easy for Marty to get into Biff's penthouse—especially with Biff distracted the way he was. He was sitting in the hot tub with a couple of well-built young women, one blond, one redhead. Marty guessed they were showgirls from Biff's Pleasure Paradise. And Biff and the showgirls were all more or less watching some Clint Eastwood movie on a big screen TV.

"Aim for the heart," Clint murmured, "or you'll never stop me."

Ramone kept on firing.

Marty had seen this movie before. *A Fistful of Dol-*

lars, wasn't it? The bullets didn't do anything to Eastwood, because he was wearing some kind of armor.

The women on either side of Biff giggled when Clint showed off the metal hiding under his sarapé.

Clint wasted another four guys. He didn't even break a sweat.

"Great flick" Biff murmured between puffs on his cigar. "Great friggin' flick."

"When the man with the forty-five," Clint said to Ramone, "meets the man with the rifle, you said the man without the rifle is a dead man. Let's see if that's true."

The screen went black.

"Hey!" Biff ejaculated. "What the hell—"

Marty stepped out from behind the giant screen, where he had finally found the controls.

"Party's over, Biff," he said with a smile.

You!" Biff demanded, waving his finger at Marty. "What are you doing here? How the hell did you get in here, anyway? How'd you get past my security downstairs?"

Marty just kept on smiling. "I managed."

"Well, you got just ten seconds to get your ass the hell out of here, or you're gonna have to be carried out!" Biff reached past the redhead and picked up the phone.

No. This was going too fast. Marty still needed to get some information.

"There's a little matter I need to talk to you about," he added hurriedly.

"Money, right?" Biff paused in his phone call, the smile back on his face. "Well, forget it."

Marty shook his head. He had to be all business now.

"Not money, no." He paused in what he hoped was a properly dramatic fashion. *"Grey's Sports Almanac,"* he added a moment later.

Biff stared at him.

"You know what I'm talking about," Marty went on, slowly and deliberately. "It's a book. Paperback, silver cover and jacket, with red letters, and pictures of a baseball player, a football player, a basketball player, and a jockey."

Biff put the phone down.

"You heard him girls," he said, not taking his eyes off Marty. "Party's over."

Both women giggled as they climbed from the hot tub. Biff watched them as they left the room, then turned back to Marty.

He pushed himself out of the tub and grabbed a robe. "C'mon, kid. Let's go talk where it's private."

Marty followed Biff into his private office. Biff went behind the desk. Marty looked down at the coffee table next to him. It was piled high with matchbooks.

"Biff's Pleasure Paradise," the kid read aloud. Black letters on a white matchbook. "Very cute."

Biff scowled back at him. Apparently, he didn't have time for cute.

"Start talkin', kid. What else do you know about that book?"

Marty stuck the matchbook in his pocket. Biff

was playing right into his hands. Now, if he could just get him to tell a little bit more.

"First," Marty demanded, "you tell me how you got it. How, when, where—"

Biff stared at him for another minute.

"All right," he agreed at last. He stood up and turned to the oil painting behind him—a full-size portrait of Biff, as if he were royalty or something.

He swung the painting out on its hinges, revealing the wall safe behind.

"November 12, 1955," he called over his shoulder as he started on the first of the three combination locks. "That was when."

"1955?" Marty asked. It couldn't be! "November 12, 1955? But that's the day I went—" He stopped himself, confused. His nerves were showing.

"I mean," Marty started again, "that was the date of the big lightning storm!"

Biff nodded, setting to work on the second lock.

"You know your history. Very good. I'll never forget that Saturday. I was pickin' up my car from the shop, 'cause I rolled it in a drag race a few days earlier."

Drag race? Marty almost laughed.

"I thought you crashed it into a manure truck."

Biff stopped and glanced back at Marty.

"How do you know about that?"

Uh-oh. He shouldn't know about that, should he? Marty grinned a little sheepishly.

"Oh—uh—my father told me about it—uh—before he died."

Biff grunted and went back to opening the third lock.

So he bought it. Good. Marty had almost blown it. It wouldn't do to let Biff in on all Marty knew.

"Well," Biff continued, "there I was, mindin' my own business, and this crazy old codger with a cane shows up. He says he's my distant relative. I don't know if he is; he doesn't even look like me." The last tumbler clicked into place. Biff reached for the safe handle. "So, he says, 'How would you like to be rich?' I says, 'sure,' so he lays this book on me."

Biff opened the safe. He pulled a box from the center shelf, then dug a key out of his pocket and unlocked the box. He grinned and pulled the sports almanac out for Marty to see.

Marty had to admit it: The book didn't look like much, unless you knew what it was—especially now that it had seen thirty years of wear and tear. The dusk jacket was gone, the pages were worn and turning yellow, there were even a couple of what looked like mustard stains on the spine.

Biff handed the book over to him so that Marty could get a closer look. Marty couldn't believe it. Biff was actually giving it to him!

"He says this book will tell me the outcome of every sporting event till the end of the century," Biff continued. "All I have to do is bet on the winner, and I'll never lose." He chuckled. "Naturally, I think he's full of it. So I say, 'What's the catch?' And he says, 'No catch. Just keep it a secret.' Then he says, 'Biff Tannen, you're one lucky guy.' After that, he disappeared and I never saw him again."

Without warning, Biff plucked the sports almanac

out of Marty's hands. Marty realized he should have turned and run while he had the chance, but he had been in a bit of shock, to actually see the book.

It was too late now. Biff had already stuck the book back in its box, and put the box on its shelf in the safe, then closed and locked the door. Apparently, show-and-tell was over. He turned back to Marty.

"Oh," he added, almost as an afterthought. He casually opened his desk drawer. "The old man told me one more thing. He said someday a crazy, wild-eyed scientist or a kid may show up asking about this book. And if that ever happens—"

Biff pulled a .38 out of the drawer and pointed it straight at Marty's head.

"Funny," Biff confessed, "I never thought it would be you."

A gun? Marty hadn't expected a gun.

"Yeah," he said shakily, "well, you're forgetting one—" Marty's jaw dropped open as he pointed to Biff's left. "Hey, look!"

Biff jerked his head around, and Marty started to run. Thank goodness Biff still fell for that one.

Biff looked back, and Marty threw a Frisbee-shaped ashtray at him. Biff ducked as Marty ran for the door.

Biff pulled the trigger, once, twice, three times. Bottles and glasses smashed on the bar as Marty ducked the gunfire. But Marty was out of there!

He heard Biff yell into the phone as he ran down the hall.

"Marty McFly's on his way down. Take care of him—permanently."

• Chapter
Fourteen •

So he didn't have the sports almanac, Marty realized. He didn't really need it, at least not now. Instead, Marty had found out exactly what he needed to know. Now all he needed to do was live long enough to use it.

By tossing that ashtray at Biff, Marty had thrown the older man off-balance long enough to get out of his office. Now what?

He ran down the corridor beyond Biff's office. It was too risky to take one of the elevators. Marty decided to try the stairs.

He opened the door that led to the stairwell. There was a soft gong sound behind him, the kind of sound an elevator made when it had arrived at your floor!

Marty jumped behind the door. As the door slid slowly closed, he could peak through the crack between door and wall to see Biff's three thugs come out of the elevator. They saw the door closing, too, and walked straight toward him!

They opened the door, with Marty still behind it. He sucked in his stomach and held his breath. If only they didn't look back here!

Marty had an idea. He dug as quietly as he could into his pocket, and pulled out a quarter, then threw it into the stairwell. It clattered as it fell.

"Hey!" one of the thugs yelled. All three of them ran down the stairs.

Marty waited for them to get down a couple of flights before he stepped from behind the doors. Then he took the steps, going up.

Maybe the plan Doc and he had cooked up would work, after all.

It was wild up on the roof, like another world.

There was plenty of light up here, but it was all pink and green, spill-off from the huge neon signs on the front of the Pleasure Paradise. There was a lot of smoke up here, too—pollution, Marty imagined, from all those smokestacks. It rolled across the roof, illuminated by the neon into a kind of pastel fog.

He walked to the edge of the roof.

Whoa!

It was twenty-eight stories, straight down.

"Go ahead, kid," a gruff voice called behind him. "Jump. A suicide'll be nice and neat."

Marty spun around. Biff had found him. He must

have heard Marty go up the stairs. And Biff still had his gun.

"Yeah?" Marty called back with a defiance he really didn't feel. "And what if I don't?"

Biff waved his gun with a smile. "Lead poisoning."

Marty glanced back over the edge of the roof—twenty-eight stories of air. There was no place to go. If Marty was going to survive this, he would have to bluff, get Biff to hesitate, get him to make a mistake. But he'd already played that "Look out, behind you!" trick. Even Biff wasn't dumb enough to fall for that one twice. What else could he do?

Even though it was Biff, Marty decided he would try logic.

"What happens to you when the police match the bullet up to that gun?" he yelled.

That only made Biff laugh.

"Kid, I *own* the police. Besides, they couldn't match up the bullet that killed your old man."

His old man? What was Biff saying? Biff had shot his father?

"I suppose it's poetic justice," Biff smirked. "Two McFlys with one gun."

Biff raised his revolver, taking careful aim.

Marty looked over the edge again. There was only one thing he could do.

He jumped from the roof before Biff could shoot. The last thing he saw was Biff's open mouth as he leaped into the air.

Biff laughed. Then he ran to the edge of the roof

to see the splattered remains of Marty McFly twenty-eight stories below.

Only Biff didn't see Marty McFly splattered. He saw him alive, suddenly rising up in midair: Marty was standing on the hood of the DeLorean.

Biff stared in astonishment. He raised his gun . . . but Doc whipped open his gull-wing door and whacked Biff in the jaw with it, giving him a mouthful of stainless steel! The impact sent Biff reeling backward; his skull slammed into the cement surface of the hotel roof and knocked him senseless.

Marty sighed with relief. Their plan had worked—just barely, but it had worked! Doc maneuvered the flying DeLorean around to the edge of the roof so that Marty could climb off the hood, open the passenger door, and get into the seat beside Doc.

With Marty safely inside, Doc flew them away from Biff's hotel.

"What's our destination time?" Doc asked.

"You won't believe it, Doc," Marty replied. "November 12, 1955."

Doc looked as if he had seen a ghost. "November 12, 1955? Great Scott! The date of the storm!" He shook his head. "Unbelievable that old Biff would have chosen that particular date. It could mean that that point in time inherently contains some sort of cosmic significance—almost as if it were a temporal junction point for the entire space-time continuum."

He paused to shrug. "On the other hand," he

added brightly, "it could be an amazing coincidence!"

"So, Doc," Marty added, "I guess we have to bring Jennifer and Einstein back with us to 1955?"

"No," Doc replied. "Assuming we succeed in our mission, we'll return to the same 1985 which we left this morning. Jennifer and Einie will still be here, and they'll be fine."

Marty frowned. Doc's theory sounded fine, but still . . .

"And if we don't succeed?" Marty asked.

"We must succeed," Doc answered simply.

It took the scientist only a minute to set the destination display. And then they were gone.

Back to November 12, 1955.

There were the usual sonic booms, and they were cruising over the fancy billboard—with all the pennants flying around it—announcing the future home of "Lyon Estates—Live in the home of tomorrow . . . today!" This was close to where Marty had shown up the first time he'd gone into the past.

It was still night as Doc landed the DeLorean behind the billboard, but Marty thought he saw a faint pink glow in the eastern sky.

So here they were, back in 1955.

But how were they going to get the book?

"All right, Marty," Doc explained, gently patting the fender. "I'm going to stay here with the DeLorean. We can't risk anyone else stealing it."

"Yeah," Marty replied, recalling his first trip here. "That farmer Peabody lives a mile down the road."

He chuckled softly. "I'd hate to think what would happen if he got his hands on it."

Doc glanced at his watch with a frown. "Sunrise should be in about twenty-two minutes. You go into town, track down young Biff, and tail him. Sometime today, old Biff will show up to give young Biff the almanac. Above all, you must not interfere with that event. We must let old Biff believe he's succeeded, so that he'll leave 1955 and bring the DeLorean back to the future." He paused to make sure Marty had gotten all that.

Marty nodded, and Doc continued, "Once old Biff is gone, you can make your move. Grab the almanac any way that you can, then come back here with it and we'll go home."

He gave Marty's shoulder a pat of encouragement. "Remember, both our lives depend on this!"

"You don't have to remind me, Doc," Marty replied. That whole business with Biff, and what had happened to Doc and Marty's whole family in that other 1985, was still much too fresh in his mind. Marty would do just about anything to keep that future from happening!

Doc went back to rummaging around in the space behind the seats. He pulled out a couple things and handed them to Marty.

"Here's some binoculars, and a walkie-talkie so we can keep in contact."

Both items were small enough for Marty to stick in his pockets. Doc looked about uncertainly. Was there something else?

Doc frowned to himself for an instant, then snapped his fingers and nodded.

"And you'll need money—" He lifted his hawaiian shirt to reveal a money belt with close to a dozen different pouches. And each pouch had a label: 1985; 1955; 2015; 1921; 1882; gold; silver; doubloons.

"I have to be prepared for all monetary possibilities," Doc explained. He reached into the 1955 pouch and pulled out a wad of bills. He handed them to Marty.

"Get yourself some fifties clothes," Doc instructed. "Something inconspicuous."

Marty was ready. He'd found a secondhand store on the edge of town that opened early, where he had picked up a cool Marlon Brando-type black leather jacket, a real Frank Sinatra porkpie hat, and a pair of sunglasses. No one would know him now! Then he checked out the phone book and found Biff's home address. Luckily there was only one Tannen in town. But the house didn't look right, somehow.

He pressed the talk button on his walkie-talkie.

"Yo, Doc! I'm at the address—it's the only Tannen in the phone book. But this can't be Biff's house. It looks like some old lady lives here."

At least, that's all he heard coming from the house, some old lady yelling all sorts of things.

Marty pulled out his binoculars to get a closer look. He could see a lot more detail this way, like the fact that the house really needed painting, and all those signs all over the yard. Marty read them one by one:

KEEP OFF THE GRASS!

What grass? From the few scruffy yellow strands left in the dirt, it looked like the lawn had died years ago.

But there were other signs, forbidding just about everything else.

NO PARKING!

NO TRESPASSING!

VIOLATORS WILL BE PROSECUTED!

THIS MEANS YOU!

And finally, slightly smaller, and behind all the others:

TANNEN

Yep, on second thought, this was just the sort of place Biff Tannen would come from.

The front door opened and Biff walked out.

"Biff!" the elderly woman's voice called from inside the Tannen house. "Where are you going, Biff?"

Biff started to walk quickly away from the house.

"To get my car, Grandma!" he called over his shoulder.

"But when are you coming back, precious?" his grandma whined. "My feet hurt, and I want you to rub my toes some more. And put polish on them!

Biff waved violently back at the house.

Marty called back to Doc on the walkie-talkie, "Never mind, Doc. Biff lives here, all right."

Marty signed off.

Biff walked rapidly toward the street.

There were a bunch of kids playing catch in the yard next door, a yard that still had a lawn. One of the kids overthrew the ball they were tossing around. It bounced into Biff's yard, rolling to his feet in the dirt and weeds.

Biff picked up the ball and kept on walking. All five kids ran over to the teenager and looked up expectantly.

"This your ball?" Biff asked with a grin.

The kids all nodded eagerly.

Biff looked from one kid to the next, all around the circle, then tossed the ball onto the roof of the house next door.

"Well, go get it!" Biff guffawed loudly as the kid's faces fell, and walked out onto the street.

So Biff had gone for his car. This was it then. Marty decided he'd better call Doc and report.

He looked out over the wide open spaces. It was a simpler time, before cars and heavy industry. A time when you could breathe and pit yourself against the elements. A time that was just right for Doc Brown, the fastest gun in the west!

He turned to look at the homestead behind him, then took a moment to pat his trusty horse.

"Yo, Doc!" his horse said. "Come in, Doc!"

Wait a moment. Why was his horse talking? Even worse, why was his horse talking with the voice of Marty McFly?

Doc opened his eyes.

"Come in, Doc!" Marty's voice crackled on the walkie-talkie. "Are you there?"

Doc sat up quickly, and reached for the radio's talk button. He must have dozed off there for a minute.

"Check, Marty," he replied, stifling a yawn. "I'm here, ever vigilant."

"Biff just left his house," Marty reported. "I'm tailing him. No sign of old Biff yet."

Doc stretched a little, trying to get a couple kinks out of his back. A DeLorean wasn't the most comfortable place to sleep in the world. He spoke into the walkie-talkie again.

"Roger. Ten-four, Marty. Keep me posted on all consequential developments. Signing off."

He yawned and tossed the walkie-talkie over on the passenger seat, then let his head fall back again against the headrest. These DeLoreans did have comfortable headrests. He would close his eyes for just another minute or two. This time travel could really tire a scientist out!

Biff had walked all the way into Courthouse Square—the real Courthouse Square, the way Marty remembered it from 1955. And Marty had followed him all the way, trying to keep enough distance between them while not losing Biff around a turn or down a side street. So far, he didn't think Biff had looked back once.

A tow truck was just pulling up in front of Western Auto, Biff's 1940 Ford Convertible hanging off the back. The car looked almost as good as it had in front of the Biff Tannen Museum—certainly a lot better than when it had hit the manure truck!

A guy in mechanic's overalls got out of the cab of the truck and walked around to disconnect Biff's car from the tow. The circular patch over his pocket said his name was Terry.

Marty stared at him: The mechanic looked familiar somehow. And then he remembered—this was the old guy who had asked him for a donation to "Save the clock tower" in the future! Of course, he was sixty years younger here in 1955, but, yes, it was the same man. Marty remembered the guy had connected the clock tower lightning storm with repairing Biff's car, and now here it was, happening right in front of him.

"Here she is, Biff," Terry gestured proudly, "all fixed up, like new. Except we couldn't get her started." He glanced over at the eager Tannen. "You got a kill switch on this thing?"

Tannen grinned at that.

"Nope, you just gotta have the right touch," he bragged. "Ain't nobody can start this car but me."

He climbed in the car and turned the key. The car growled to life on the first try.

The mechanic nodded distractedly, as if he was slightly impressed. He pulled a clipboard out of his truck and checked the paper work.

"Let's see," he said as he read the paper before him. "The bill comes to three-hundred and two dollars and fifty-seven cents."

Biff turned a shade of red almost as deep as the Western Auto sign.

"Three-hundred bucks?" he screamed. "Three-hundred bucks? For a couple of dents? That's bullshit, Terry!"

"Actually," Terry replied in a bored tone, as if he had expected Biff's temper tantrum all along, "it was horseshit. The car was full of it. We even found some in the glove compartment. We had so much manure piled up in the service bay, we had to pay old man Jones eighty bucks to haul it away."

Biff laughed nastily.

"Yeah, and I'll bet the old skinflint resold it, too. I oughta get something for that!"

Terry the mechanic turned toward the store. He waved for Biff to follow him.

"C'mon," Terry said, "let's write you up inside."

Biff cut the engine and climbed out of the car.

"Three-hundred bucks!" he continued loudly. "I'll tell you, Terry, if I ever get my hands on that son of a bitch who caused this, I'll break his neck!"

Marty had to grin at that. As the son of a bitch that Biff was talking about, he had to admit it—it was all sorts of fun to get Biff Tannen pissed off. As long, Marty added, as Biff didn't have a gun.

Biff and Terry disappeared inside the store. In another minute, Marty imagined, Biff would come back out and drive away—and there was no way Marty could follow him on foot. There was only one thing to do, then.

Marty would have to hide in the back of Biff's car.

• Chapter
Fifteen •

Marty crouched in the backseat of Biff's car. This early in the morning, there was hardly anyone around in Hill Valley, and it had been easy for him to jump in the car without being noticed. He cautiously peeked over the front seat and saw Biff come out of Western Auto, carrying half a dozen cans of oil.

Marty ducked down in the well between the seats. Now, as long as Biff didn't look back here . . .

He felt half a dozen oil cans get dumped on his back. As much as it hurt, he suffered it in silence. Now, as long as Biff didn't look where he had thrown things . . .

"Well, well," Biff said loudly, "lookee what we have here!"

For a second, Marty thought Biff had spotted him.

But then he realized Biff's voice was growing fainter. Biff was moving away from the car.

What was going on? Marty couldn't stand it. The oil cans rolled toward his feet as he lifted his head to peek out again.

Marty's mother, Lorraine, had just come out of Ruth's Frock Shop. Marty recognized her dark-haired best friend, Babs, too. This being 1955, of course, Lorraine was still a teenager, just about Marty's age. She was carrying a new dress with her—a dress, Marty remembered, that she would wear to tonight's dance.

Biff had gone over to talk to the girls. "Hey, nice dress, Lorraine." He smirked at the two of them. "Although I think you'd look better wearin' nothin' at all."

Lorraine rolled her eyes heavenward. "Biff, why don't you take a long walk off a short pier!"

She and Babs started to walk away. Biff followed.

"Hey," he protested, "I'm just trying to make polite conversation."

"You heard her," Babs broke in. "Make like a banana and split."

"I ain't talkin' to you!" Biff snapped. He turned to the other girl. "Listen Lorraine, there's that dance at school tonight. Now that my car's all fixed, I figured I'd cut you a break and give you the honor of goin' with the best lookin' guy in school."

Lorraine stopped and looked up at the still smirking boy.

"Kind of short notice, isn't it, Biff?"

Biff shrugged generously. "Hey, I'm a spontaneous guy."

Lorraine nodded curtly and started to walk again.

"Yeah, well, I'm busy."

Biff stepped in front of her so she couldn't leave.

"Yeah? What could be more important than going out with me?"

Lorraine glanced at Babs.

"Washing my hair."

Babs started to giggle.

"Oh," Biff replied angrily, "that's about as funny as a screen door on a battleship!"

"Submarine, you idiot," Marty muttered to himself. A screen door on a submarine! Biff could never get those sayings right!

"Look, Biff," Lorraine said patiently, "I've already been asked to the dance."

"By who?" Biff demanded. "That bug, George McFly?"

Lorraine frowned at Biff's suggestion, her patience at an end.

"I'm going with Calvin Klein, okay?"

She meant Marty, of course. That Calvin Klein name was the one he'd gone by last time he was here. Lorraine had called him that when she had seen the name sewn into his underwear; and Marty had figured that, since he couldn't very well go by his own name—McFly—"Calvin Klein" would have to do.

But Biff went crazy when Lorraine mentioned that

name. He grabbed Lorraine's arm and dragged her toward him.

"No, it's not okay!" he screamed. "You're going with me, understand?"

Whoa, Marty thought. Temper, temper. All this because the guy Biff knew as Calvin Klein had made him run his car into a manure truck?

"Get your hands off me!" Lorraine shouted back.

Biff was hurting her! Marty wanted to go out there and give Biff some of his own medicine. But he couldn't show himself to Biff now! That might blow the whole thing, and he'd never find the sports almanac!

Lorraine tried to pull away, but Biff wouldn't let go. Both of Marty's hands balled into fists without him even thinking about it. He couldn't just sit here and watch this. Marty bit his knuckle. His mother was always telling him not to fight—not to let the others goad him into something by calling him "chicken." She always wanted him to count to ten. Well, he would, this time, for his mother. But if Biff was still manhandling Lorraine by the time he was done, Marty would *have* to go out and stop it—no matter what else happened!

One . . . two . . .

"When are you gonna get it through your thick skull, Lorraine?" Biff demanded. "You're *my* girl!"

Five . . . six . . .

"Biff Tannen," she spat back, "I wouldn't be your girl even if you had a million dollars!"

With that, she stomped on his foot.

Biff let go with a gasp, then Lorraine bashed him in the head with the dress box.

Lorraine and Babs quickly walked down the street.

Marty let out all the air he had been holding in. He was glad that was over.

Oh, shit! There was somebody else getting into the front seat of the car.

Marty ducked down quick, hoping he hadn't been noticed.

"Oh yes, you will!" Biff half shouted, half groaned through his pain. "It's you and me, Lorraine! It's meant to be! You're gonna marry me someday, Lorraine! You're gonna be my wife!"

Marty shivered as he thought about that other 1985, when Biff's words had come true. He'd do almost anything to make sure that didn't happen again. But who had gotten in the car? Marty looked up at the driver's seat, and saw a head of white hair.

It was old Biff, from the future! This must be the moment they first met, when old Biff gave his younger self the sports almanac!

"You always did have a way with women," old Biff cackled.

"Hey!" his younger self hollered. "Get the hell out of my car, old man!"

But old Biff only laughed again.

"You wanna marry that girl, Biff? I can help you make it happen."

"Yeah?" Biff asked sarcastically. "Who are you, Miss Lonelyhearts?"

Old Biff sighed.

"Get in the car, butthead," he ordered.

"Who you callin' butthead, butthead?" the youngster shot back.

Marty heard the engine catch, then come to life with a roar. Old Biff must have started the car.

"How'd you know how to do that?" the younger Biff demanded. "Nobody can start my car except me."

"Just get in, Tannen," old Biff ordered. "Today's your lucky day."

There was a moment's silence, then the sound of footsteps and a door opening and closing. The teenager had decided to get into the car.

Old Biff eased the old Ford forward.

Marty let out a deep breath. So far, he thought, so good.

When he decided to hide in the back of Biff's roadster, he never guessed he would have both Biffs in the front seat. But, up till now at least, neither one of them had looked back. The way they were jawing up there now, Marty hoped they wouldn't have time to look at anything else.

A couple of minutes passed, then the car drove out of the sunlight and stopped. Old Biff turned off the engine. Marty looked up and saw rafters overhead. They must be in Biff's garage.

"How'd you know where I live?" the younger Biff demanded.

"I know a lot about you, Biff," the older version replied smugly. "For example, I know you'd like to make a lot of money."

"Yeah, so?" the teenager mumbled, obviously not impressed. "Who wouldn't?"

"Could be," old Biff went on slyly, "I'm the guy to show you how."

"Sure, right. Who are you supposed to be, pops? My fairy godmother?"

Marty thought the young Biff would be surprised to know just how right he was.

"Let's just say we're related, Biff," the older version answered. "And, that being the case, I've got a little present for you."

There was a rustling up in the front seat. This was it! Old Biff was going to show him the almanac!

"See this book?" old Biff continued. "This book will tell you the outcome of every major sports event till the end of the century. All you have to do is bet on the winner, and you'll never lose."

"That's very nice," the teenager replied, as if he was sure now that the old man was crazy. "Thank you very much." His voice gained a hard edge as he added, "Now why don't you just make like a tree and get outta here!"

"It's 'leave' you idiot!" old Biff shouted back at him. " 'Make like a tree and leave!' You sound like a damned fool when you say it wrong!"

"Fine!" the teenager snapped, still not convinced. "And take your book with you!"

But old Biff wouldn't leave.

"Sure," he insisted sarcastically, "be a butthead and be poor for the rest of your life. But you could be rich. You could buy anything you want. Have any girl you want. You could own this town." He paused for a minute, like a guy who had hooked the fish and was just waiting to reel it in. "All you gotta do is bet on the winners."

There was a crackle of static. For one, panicked second, Marty thought Doc was calling him on the walkie-talkie. The Biffs would hear; he'd be discovered; everything would be lost.

And then Marty realized one of the Biffs had turned on the radio. He heard a couple of blasts of music as somebody fiddled with the dial, then the sound of a crowd—the kind of noise you always heard in the background of a baseball or football game.

"Five yard penalty on UCLA," the radio sportscaster announced, "pushing them back to the Washington nineteen yard line. UCLA trails, seventeen to sixteen. It's fourth and eleven with only forty-eight seconds remaining in this game. The Bruins have not looked good today, and I'd say that Washington has pulled off the biggest upset of the season!"

Marty could hear the sound of pages turning.

"He's wrong," old Biff said authoritatively. "UCLA's gonna win it—nineteen to seventeen."

"What, are you deaf, old man?" the younger Biff asked. "He just said it was over!"

"Here's the snap by Palmer to Bradley," the sportscaster said, even louder than before. Marty realized old Biff must have turned up the radio. "Decker back to place-kick formation. Here comes

Decker with the kick, it looks good folks, it looks very good—

"Field goal!" the announcer screamed over the roar of the crowd. "Nineteen to seventeen, UCLA and this Coliseum crowd is going wild! A perfect thirty-five-yard kick for senior halfback Jim Decker, with less than eighteen seconds remaining, wins this game for UCLA!" The announcer's voice dropped an octave. "And Bob, I wonder what the odds of something like this happening are?"

"Speaking of odds, Bill," a different voice replied, "UCLA was a twenty-point favorite to win this game." Bob chuckled. 'I sure wish I'd taken a point spread on this one. I could have made a small fortune! I tell you, Bill—"

"You here that, Biff?" the oldster asked triumphantly as he turned off the radio. "If you'd have bet on this game, you'd have cleaned up! *Now*, would you like to have this book?"

"Okay, pops," the young Biff answered, a touch of awe in his voice. "I'll take a look at it. But it sounds crazy to me."

"Check it against the sports page tomorrow," the senior citizen insisted, "and then decide if it's crazy."

Something went thunk on the backseat of the car. Marty looked up. It was the sports book! Biff must have tossed it back here after his older self gave it to him. All Marty had to do was reach out and grab . . .

A liver-spotted hand closed over the book and snatched it away.

"You damned fool!" old Biff yelled. "Never leave this book lying around! Don't you have a safe?" The old man made a disgusted sound deep in his throat. "No, you don't have a safe. Get a safe! Keep the book locked up! And until then, keep the book on you! Like this!"

Marty could hear old Biff stuffing the book some place or other. Car doors opened and closed. They were getting out!

"And don't ever tell anybody about it, either," old Biff continued, his voice growing fainter as the two walked away. "Oh, there's one more thing."

Marty got up cautiously to peek over the top of the seat.

"Someday, a kid or a weird-looking old man . . ." Old Biff's voice faded as the two of them disappeared around the corner.

Marty waited a minute. Once they were away from the garage, he would get out of the car and follow them.

Young Biff stepped back in front of the doorway. Marty ducked down. He heard a creaking sound, like old hinges complaining. It was getting much darker in here.

Marty risked another look. Biff was closing the garage doors! The two doors slammed together as Marty lifted his head to watch, followed—immediately—by a heavy click.

Marty didn't like the sound of that click.

He got out of the car and moved to the doors. He tried to tug them open, but they wouldn't budge.

He pulled harder, hoping they were stuck, but they didn't move at all. They weren't stuck. Biff had locked them. That click meant there was a padlock on the other side.

He looked around the garage. The windows were tiny. They let in hardly any light at all, and they were too small for even a child to get through. Marty was trapped in here!

And it was worse than that. Not only had old Biff given his younger self the book, he had warned the teenager of the book's true importance. What if the young Biff did go out and get a safe—how could Doc and Marty get the book back then? And the longer Biff was left alone with the book, the more chance he had to use it. Once Biff started to win, would part—or all—of that terrible, Biff-controlled future be inevitable?

Marty had to stop that from happening at almost any cost, not just for his family and friends, but all of Hill Valley.

There was only one thing left to do. He pulled the walkie-talkie from his jacket pocket and pressed the talk button.

"Doc!" he spoke softly but clearly, in case either of the Biffs were still around.

The speaker on Marty's box crackled with a burst of static. "Marty!" Doc's voice came through a second later. "What's the report?"

"Biff has the book, the old man is gone, and I'm locked in Biff's garage!" Marty replied succinctly.

"Great Scott!" Doc answered.

"You've got to come and get me out!" Marty insisted. He dug in his pocket, and retrieved the piece of paper where he had written down Biff's address when he got it from the phone book. "The address is 2311 Mason Street."

"Mason Street?" Doc protested. "But that's way over on the other side of town! I can't drive the DeLorean there in the daylight!"

And Biff would get away with the sports book! "Then walk, run, just get here any way you can, Doc!"

"All right, Marty!" Doc replied. "I'm coming."

He just hoped Doc would get here in time.

• Chapter
Sixteen •

Marty paced back and forth like a caged animal. He had been locked in this garage for hours. It had gotten dark outside while he waited. What could be taking Doc so long?

Someone banged on the outside of the garage door.

"Doc?" Marty called softly.

But the voice that answered wasn't Doc's.

"Who's in there?" Biff demanded angrily.

Jeez, now Marty had done it. He heard Biff unlock the padlock. Marty looked around the garage. Messy as it was, there was no place to hide in here. No place, that is, except for the floor of the backseat of the convertible.

Marty jumped in the back of the car just as Biff opened the door. He caught a glimpse of the other teen as he ducked out of sight. Biff had changed clothes. He now wore a black shirt, white tie, and gray jacket, clothes that looked somehow familiar. Of course! Marty remembered. It was the night of the "Enchantment Under the Sea" dance.

"Is somebody in here?" Biff yelled. Marty could hear his footsteps on the concrete floor.

There was a burst of static from Marty's walkie-talkie.

Marty yanked it from his pocket and turned the radio off. But the damage was done. Biff must have heard that.

Biff walked past the car.

"Old man," he called uncertainly, "are you still in here?"

Marty glanced up at Biff's retreating backside. There, shoved in Biff's waistband, was the sports almanac!

Marty heard laughter outside the garage.

Biff stopped, and then walked quickly out into the driveway.

"Dammit, you kids!" Biff yelled out into the darkness. "If I see you around here again, I'll kill you both!"

Marty crouched down again as Biff stomped heavily back into the garage and got behind the wheel. Marty lifted himself up enough to see that Biff had put the almanac down on the dashboard.

Now, if there was just some way he could reach it . . .

He ducked down quickly as Biff threw the car into reverse and gunned it back out of the driveway.

Somehow, Marty had to get that book. It was up to him now.

But what had happened to Doc?

Well, it had taken him a little while, and he had had to swerve at the last minute to avoid getting hit by that hot-rodding teenager, but he was here at last.

Doc wheeled the bike he'd bought a few hours ago into the driveway of 2311 Mason Street. That was the address Marty had given him? Yes, it definitely checked with what Doc had written down in his notebook. But then why was the garage door—the door Marty was supposed to be trapped behind—now sitting open?

Doc supposed this had something to do with how long it took him to get here. Well, it *had* taken him a little while to buy the bike, after he had figured out that was the best thing to do with what 1955 money he had left. Why, he hadn't even taken the price tag off the bike, he had been in such a hurry. But then, of course, he'd needed to buy this hat he was wearing, for disguise purposes, of course. Well, it wasn't much of a disguise, just a hat, but then, Doc hadn't had much time to buy it.

Even then, though, he would have gotten here earlier if he had been able to take a more direct route. He sighed. That was one of the problems with time traveling. A couple of the roads he had expected to take to get here hadn't been built yet. And then his muscles had started to complain. That was another trouble with all this time travel—when you sat in a DeLorean all day long, you ended up neglecting much-needed exercise!

So he was a little late. He hoped Marty would understand. That is, if the lad was still here.

Doc pedaled right into the garage. There didn't seem to be anybody around.

"Marty?" he called. "Marty?"

Doc realized then that Biff's car was gone, too. Marty must have gotten out of here somehow. Maybe he had hidden in the back of Biff's car or something, and was once again on the trail of the sports almanac.

But that meant Marty could be anywhere in Hill Valley! Doc decided to try the walkie-talkie. He pulled the box from his pocket and pushed the "speak" button.

"Marty, come in?"

There was no response. He tried it again. Still nothing.

"Damn!" What could have happened to the boy? Could he be out of walkie-talkie range? Could something be wrong with his two-way radio?

Doc decided it was useless to conjecture when he had insufficient information. Instead, he decided he would broadcast a message anyway, just in case Marty could hear him but couldn't reply.

"Marty," he said into the walkie-talkie, "if you receive this message, I'm at the garage, but I've obviously missed you. Therefore, I am returning to the DeLorean! Contact me when you can! Over and out!"

There was still no reply, and nothing else he could do. Doc turned the bike around and started the long ride back across town.

Could Marty risk it?

Once Biff had gotten out of his driveway, he had turned the radio up, loud, and then floored it, so that the car was really moving. Marty decided he had to try. Between the radio and the air rushing by the open convertible top, Biff shouldn't be able to hear anything going on in the backseat at all. Should he?

Marty pulled out the walkie-talkie and flipped it on.

"Yo, Doc!" he called softly. "Come in, Doc!"

"Hello?" Doc's voice replied. "Marty? Come in?"

Doc's voice was followed by an incredibly loud burst of static. Biff half-turned toward the backseat with a "What the—" expression on his face. He must have heard that! Marty turned the walkie-talkie down—way down. Biff looked back at the convertible's radio and started to fiddle with the knobs. Marty realized with relief that Biff must have thought the static came from up there. Biff ended up turning the radio up even louder.

Maybe, Marty thought, he should try to contact Doc again. He decided to wait a minute first—he didn't want any more sudden noises to make Biff suspicious. He had to stay as inconspicuous as possible, until he could get the sports book.

• • •

Marty wasn't answering his radio again. He must be somewhere where it was difficult to talk. Doc stuck his walkie-talkie back in his pocket. He would have to concentrate on his pedaling for now and hope that, if Marty called again, there would be something he could do to help.

"Great Scott!" Doc exclaimed. He'd been so busy talking to Marty, he hadn't realized where he had pedaled to.

He stopped the bike and stared.

He was in Courthouse Square, on that night in 1955 when this whole thing had begun. There it was in front of him, all the parts of the so-called "lightning experiment"—in reality a setup to return Marty and the time machine back where they belonged, in 1985. If only he had left well enough alone after that! Oh well. It was no use cursing crossed wires. They had already saved themselves, and members of Marty's family, more than once by using time travel. They would get through these problems, too—somehow.

In the meantime, though, he was here, at the sight of his first great triumph. Now, the sooner he got back to the DeLorean, the better, but—it wouldn't hurt to relive this experience for just a minute, would it? As he recalled, it was Thomas Wolfe who had said, "You can't go home again." Well, maybe you couldn't, but if you had a time machine, you could get awfully damn close!

There it was, the wire running down from the clock tower to the lamppost, and the toolbox on the trailer, sitting next to the DeLorean hidden under the tarpaulin. It gave Doc a thrill just to see everything set up again. Wasn't science wonderful?

Wait a minute. There on the tarp—that was his coat, or at least the coat he wore in 1955. Well, when he was originally in 1955. Whatever. He reached his hand forward to check the pocket. Yep. The letter was in there, the one Marty had written about Doc's future. There was the envelope—"Do Not Open Until 1985!" And Doc knew enough now to leave it there.

But it was time to get back on his bike and return to the DeLorean, before something else happened.

His walkie-talkie squelched to life.

"Yo, Doc, come in!" Marty called. "Are you there?"

Doc pulled the radio out of his pocket, quickly turning the volume down. He didn't want the noise to attract any undue attention—especially around here.

"Marty!" Doc whispered into the microphone. "What happened? I went to Biff's house, but you weren't there!"

"You must have just missed me," Marty whispered back. "I'm in the back of Biff's car. He's driving to the school."

To the school? Doc didn't like the sound of that.

"Listen, Marty, we may have to abort this entire plan. It's getting much too dangerous."

"Don't worry, Doc," Marty reassured him. "The book is on Biff's dashboard. I'll be able to grab it as soon as we get to the 'Enchantment Under the Sea' dance.''

What? This was even worse!

"You're going to the dance?" he asked, his voice growing louder as panic threatened to set in. "Marty, you must be extremely careful not to run into your other self!''

"My other self?" Marty asked.

"Yes," Doc continued, "remember? Your mother is on her way to that exact same dance with *you*!''

"Oh.'' Marty's voice sounded a little surprised. "Yeah, that's right! Hey, that's cool, Doc. Maybe I'll say hello to myself.''

"No!" Doc felt like he might have a heart attack. "Marty, whatever happens, you must not let your other self see you. The consequences could be disastrous!''

"Excuse me, sir!" a voice said behind him—a voice that was disturbingly familiar. Where had he heard . . .

Doc glanced behind him and saw himself—well, a different version of himself, circa 1955—emerging from under the tarp. Yes! He remembered. He had worked inside the car on that night. And then he had—come out!

But this was terrible! Doc turned off the walkie-talkie and pulled his hat down over his head. Maybe, if he kept his back to his earlier version, the other Doc Brown would just go away.

But the other Doc Brown insisted on making contact.

"Yes," he said, even louder than before, "you there, with the hat!"

For once, Doc Brown wished he didn't always have to be so stubborn—especially when he was younger! Well, he had to do something about this, didn't he?

Maybe, he thought, if he disguised his voice . . .

"Who, me?' he asked gruffly.

"Yeah," his 1955 version answered. "Be a pal and hand me a three-eighths-inch wrench."

To tighten the flux capacitor? But that was all wrong!

"Three-eighths?" Doc replied just as gruffly as before. "Don't you mean a half-inch?"

"Why," his 1955 self said in astonishment, "you're right!"

Doc reached into the toolbox. He handed his 1955 version the correct wrench without turning around. But should he say something else? Maybe a little polite conversation would keep his younger self from getting suspicious.

"I presume," Doc added, "you're conducting some sort of weather experiment."

"That's right!" 1955 exclaimed, every bit as astonished as before. "How did you know that?"

"Oh," Doc replied humbly (but still as gruffly as his voice could stand), "I happen to have a little experience in that area."

"Yes, well," 1955 explained, pleased to find a colleague, "I'm hoping to see some lightning tonight, although the weatherman says there's not going to be any rain."

"Oh," Doc reassured him, "there'll be rain, all right. And wind, thunder, lightning—" He couldn't help but chuckle. "It's gonna be one hell of a storm."

He heard the rustle of the tarp as his 1955 self prepared to go back into the car.

"Well, nice talking to you," 1955 said. "Maybe we'll bump into each other again sometime in the future."

"Or the past," Doc added, once his younger self was gone and he was safely back on his bike.

Still, he had met his younger self, and they both had survived. He could only hope that Marty would be as lucky.

• Chapter
Seventeen •

Biff stopped the car. Even from the well behind the seat, Marty could see the upper story of the high school across the parking lot. Biff climbed out. Marty waited a minute, then cautiously raised his head so he could see over the side of the convertible.

Biff was headed for the back entrance to the gym. God! Marty thought. He never thought he would say this, but he was really glad to see Hill Valley High whole again, and not that bombed-out hulk he'd found in that other 1985.

Wait a minute! Biff had left the sports book behind. It was still sitting on the dashboard. Marty couldn't believe his luck. All he had to do was lift himself up a little bit more, then reach forward and . . .

Marty ducked as Biff turned around and headed

back toward the car. Biff grabbed the almanac, and stuck it once more in the back of his pants, then walked toward the gym again.

Marty climbed out of the car once Biff had crossed the parking area, then ran and hid behind one of the pillars by the school's back door. He knew he never should have expected this to be easy. Marty would just have to keep Biff in sight, and wait to make his move.

Biff walked quickly to a fire door at the back of the gym. A couple of other students walked over as Biff tried the door.

"Hold it there, Biff!" one of the students called.

"Yeah, Biff," the other guy added. "We can't let you in without a ticket."

Biff held his right fist up to the two other guys. "I got five tickets right here."

The other two guys took off. Biff opened the fire door, and went into the dance the back way.

Marty decided he should follow him. The two student guards were long gone, and the fire door opened easily. He stepped through, and found himself in the same alcove where he'd had that heart-to-heart with his future parents—the one about being nice when your son sets fire to the rug.

But there was no time to think about that now. He walked through another doorway and found himself at the rear of the gym, a gym all decked out for the "Enchantment Under the Sea" dance.

Marty quickly ducked into the shadows behind the refreshment table. Wow. Here he was again at that same dance—back in 1955. Talk about déjà vu! He'd been so worried about getting the sports almanac back, it hadn't hit him until now, but he was back in the *exact* same place and time he'd been— when was it? Marty realized he couldn't figure out exactly how long ago it was since he *had* been here. When you had a machine like Doc's flying DeLorean, time sort of lost its meaning.

This was the same dance that he had come to with Lorraine, when he was here as "Calvin Klein." It all happened because his mother-to-be had wound up with a crush on Calvin, and wouldn't pay attention to George, Marty's future father. But if George and Lorraine never dated, then they would never marry, and Marty and his brother and sister would never get born! Something had to be done, and fast, or Marty wouldn't have even existed!

Marty had come up with this plan for George McFly to discover Calvin trying to take advantage of Lorraine in a car. George would end up punching Calvin/Marty out, and would end up being a hero in Lorraine's eyes. George and Lorraine would fall in love and get married, Marty would get born, and everything would turn out fine.

That was the plan, anyway. But then Biff had gotten into the act, and tried to take advantage of Lorraine. So George had ended up punching Biff out! That had changed everything, for the better. At least until now.

But, Marty reminded himself grimly, unless he

could get the sports book away from Biff, everything would change all over again!

And it wasn't even as simple as that anymore. Who knew how the earlier version of Marty would react, if he happened to meet his future self face-to-face. Marty would have to be careful around George and Lorraine, too, or he could mess up everything all over again. So he had to be doubly cautious going after Biff.

He pulled out the mini-binoculars Doc had given him and scanned the room. There was George McFly, his father-to-be, standing around and looking nervous at the other end of the gym. It was early enough in the evening that "Calvin" and Lorraine wouldn't be here yet. And there, in the middle of the room, was Mr. Strickland, his bald head bobbing up and down as he prowled the dance floor for slackers. Heck, now that he no longer had his scar and shotgun, Marty was almost glad to see Mr. Strickland.

Biff was over in the other corner of the room, surrounded by his usual gang—3-D, Match, and Skinhead. They were all gathered around a couple of digest-sized magazines Biff had with him, leering at whatever was inside. Marty studied the covers with his binoculars. Their titles were in French. One of them was called *Ooh-La-La*! From the pictures on the covers, they looked like girlie magazines. Trust Biff to bring something like that to the dance. Biff pointed at some particular detail while the other guys all laughed. The four of them were also passing a small bottle of booze around, taking quick drinks whenever Strickland's back was turned.

But they hadn't been careful enough. Marty could see Strickland had stopped on the other side of the room, his beady eyes staring at Biff and his boys. Skinhead saw Strickland, too. He nudged Biff. Their leader looked up at the vice-principal, then said something to the whole gang. All four of them walked toward the front door.

Marty quickly walked around the edge of the gym, careful to keep close to the walls, but heading for the same exit. Biff and his gang had moved fast. They had already passed through the doorway. He didn't want to lose them now!

Marty stepped outside quickly, once again moving into the shadows beyond the party lights, slowly going down the front steps of the school. He stopped on the edge of the first landing. There, on the next landing below him, were Biff and his gang, with their magazines and booze.

Biff hit a picture of a naked girl with the tips of his fingers. "Y'know," he said slowly, "a smart guy could make a lot of dough dealin' this kind of stuff."

3-D drained the last of the booze from the bottle. He handed the empty to Biff.

"Drink up, Biff!" 3-D called.

Biff lifted the bottle to his lips. His eyes opened wide when he realized it was empty.

Skinhead, Match, and 3-D laughed as if that was the funniest thing they had ever seen.

Biff threw down the bottle and punched 3-D's shoulder. "That's so funny, I forgot to laugh."

He looked out over the school parking lot as couples started to climb the stairs toward the dance.

"So where's that Calvin Klein creep?"

"We don't know, Biff," Skinhead replied sarcastically. "We ain't his secretary!"

The guys started to laugh all over again.

"Well, go find him!" Biff barked angrily, killing the laughter before it could really begin.

The three stooges turned to go up the stairs again, back into the gym.

Marty spun around so that his back was to them. He didn't want to get spotted by the gang—not when he was this close!

"Ain't you comin', Biff?" Match asked.

Biff shook the girlie magazine in his hand.

"I'm readin'."

Marty continued to pivot away from the gang members as they climbed the stairs past him.

Marty found himself looking down at Biff. The burly teenager had stuck himself in a corner on the next landing, between the doorway to the high school annex and a chain link fence. Biff leaned against the fence and flipped through the magazine, grunting and snickering whenever he found anything particularly to his liking.

But, besides Biff's laughter, Marty realized, there wasn't a sound out here. His three buddies had gone back into the dance to look for "Calvin." Biff was all alone. And Marty could see the almanac, shoved in the back of Biff's pants.

Maybe it was time for Marty to make his move. He glanced around to see how many other kids were around—the fewer the better, Marty figured. This confrontation with Biff might get messy.

He stopped when he saw a yellow Packard pull into the parking area. That yellow Packard was very familiar. He pulled out his binoculars to get a closer look. Yep, there was Lorraine in the passenger seat, wearing that dress she'd bought earlier today. And he, Marty McFly, was driving. Marty was standing here, with the binoculars, watching himself. He was two places at one time.

Marty had to admit it. "This is getting strange," he whispered.

Strange or not, there was nobody else around this corner of the school yard at the moment. Marty might not get another opportunity as good as this. He had to get that book now.

He jumped from the landing, vaulting into the stairwell on the other side of the chain link fence. His feet scraped the concrete as he landed. Biff glanced behind him, but Marty had crouched down low, in the shadows. Biff went back to his magazine.

Marty crept across the stairwell. The almanac was in his reach. All he had to do was silently put out his hand and . . .

The doorway opened, and Mr. Strickland stepped out.

"Well, well, Mr. Tannen," Strickland remarked in that voice that always found you guilty until proven innocent, "how nice to see you here."

Biff looked around at the newcomer, whipping the magazine behind his back in a single fluid motion.

"Why, Mr. Strickland, sir," Biff-the-soul-of-innocence replied. "Nice to see you here, sir."

Strickland stuck his bald head right up against Biff's surprised face.

"Is that liquor I smell, Tannen?"

Biff shook his head, still as wide-eyed as before.

"I wouldn't know, sir," he answered, slowly and patiently. "I don't know what liquor smells like because I'm too young to drink it."

Strickland stared at Biff with those trained vice-principal's eyes, guaranteed to see into your soul.

"I see. And what do we have—"

Quick as a cobra, Strickland reached behind the teenager and snatched the magazine from behind Biff's back.

"—here?" he finished triumphantly.

Marty started when he saw the cover in the vice-principal's hands. Somehow, Strickland had grabbed hold of Grey's Sports Almanac!

"Sports statistics," Strickland muttered as he glanced at the cover. "Interesting subject." He opened the book and casually flipped through the pages. He raised a single eyebrow as he looked back at Biff. "Homework, Tannen?"

Biff had obviously had enough of the vice-principal. He leered and shook his head.

"No, it ain't homework," he drawled, " 'cause I ain't at home."

Strickland gave Biff one of his disciplinary shoves. "You've got a real attitude problem. You know that, Tannen?" The vice-principal stuck the sports almanac in his pocket. "Just watch it, because one day I'm gonna have you right where I want you—in detention." He pointed an accusing finger in Biff's direction. "Slacker!"

Strickland turned and marched away—and he still had the almanac!

"Butthead!" Biff yelled after the retreating disciplinarian. He started to shake his fist, then decided to go back up to the dance, instead.

Strickland was crossing the lawn, toward the school door closest to the administrative offices. Marty guessed he'd better follow him, instead.

But to tail Strickland, he had to walk right by the parking lot and the yellow Packard, with Lorraine and the other Marty both still sitting inside. Marty ducked down low as he scooted by, hoping neither of them would see him, then followed Strickland through the door to the administrative wing. He had to get that sports book before the vice-principal locked it away.

Doc could see the Lyon Estates billboard up ahead at last! His legs were heavier than lead. He felt like he'd been pedaling this bicycle all day. Come to think of it, he had been pedaling all day, hadn't he? But wait a minute. There were a couple of vehicles parked up in front of the billboard. Had someone discovered the DeLorean? Doc forgot all about the pain as the fear took over.

He pedaled twice as fast the rest of the way to the signs. As he got closer, he saw there was a pickup truck and a car parked near the sign. The side of the truck used to read: TWIN PINES RANCH, except now the "S" in pines was x-ed out, as was the word TWIN, with LONE scrawled above it. Something must have happened to one of the rancher's pine trees. Under the ranch name, in smaller letters, were the words: "Otis Peabody, Proprietor." Oh, yes. Old man Peabody, the pine tree breeder. Yes, indeed, this might be trouble. Especially because the second vehicle here was a police car!

Doc stopped his bike a few feet away.

The farmer, a thin, hyperactive sort, was waving his arms and shouting. In one hand he held a shotgun, in the other some sort of magazine.

"It was a flyin' saucer, I tell ya'!" Peabody yelled at the cop. "From Pluto! Just like this one!" He shook the periodical, which Doc realized was a comic book, titled *Tales From Space*!

The cop, a bit more heavyset and a whole lot calmer than the farmer, looked skeptical.

"I seen it come down here before dawn!" Peabody insisted.

Great Scott! Doc suddenly realized. Flying saucer? Before dawn? They must be talking about the DeLorean! But, apparently, that meant they hadn't found it yet, even though it was sitting on the other side of this very billboard!

"And I'm tellin' you, there's nothing out here, Mr. Peabody," the cop answered patiently. "It must have been your imagination."

But Peabody shook his head stubbornly. "No, sir!" he insisted. "It's around here somewhere! It's the same mutated son of a bitch that wrecked my barn last week, and I'm stayin' right here till I spot him!" He waved his shotgun at the cop. "And then I'm gonna blast him!"

Staying right here? Blast him? Not, Doc Brown thought, if he had anything to do with it. He dismounted and walked his bike forward, greeting both farmer and police officer with a friendly grin.

"You mean the flying saucer?" Doc asked helpfully. "I saw it, too! It went way over there—" Doc pointed back the way he had come. "A couple of miles!" He waved back that way to indicate the immense distance. "Way . . . out . . . there!"

Peabody grinned, happy to be in on the chase.

"Thanks, mister!" he called to Doc as he climbed into his truck. "C'mon, flatfoot, let's go!"

The cop jumped into his cruiser, and both of them took off toward town.

Doc waited until they were out of sight before he looked behind the billboard.

Yes, the DeLorean was still there.

But what could be keeping Marty?

• Chapter Eighteen •

Strickland had disappeared. The hall inside the school was deserted. But then Marty noticed there was a light on behind one of the office doors.

He crept to the door and opened it a crack. The office beyond was broken into halves by a glass partition. The half closer to Marty was where Strickland's secretary had her desk. Strickland had gone into the far end of the room, which was his office.

Marty stepped into the outer office, silently closing the door to the hallway behind him. He could see Mr. Strickland moving around behind the smoked glass. It looked like the vice-principal's back was to Marty.

Marty quickly crossed the room and tilted his head just enough so that he could see around the partition.

Strickland threw the almanac down on his desk, then sat down in his swivel chair. He opened a drawer and pulled out a whiskey bottle.

A whiskey bottle? Mr. Strickland drank? In the high school?

Strickland took a drink straight from the bottle, then swiveled his chair around so that his back was to Marty.

But how could Marty get his hands on the almanac? He couldn't very well just march in there and say, "Excuse me, Mr. Strickland," could he?

Then he saw that Strickland's desk had an open space in the middle—the place where Strickland would stick his knees—that went all the way through. If Marty could get in there—and it was only a couple feet away—without Strickland seeing him, maybe he could grab the sports book while the vice-principal's back was still turned and get out of here!

It was worth a try. He crouched down and ran into the room, dropping down on the opposite side of the desk from Strickland. He crawled into the kneehole, and saw that the disciplinarian had turned his head toward the door. Had the vice-principal heard Marty? But then Strickland shrugged and took another swig from the bottle. He looked back out the window.

Marty crawled through the space under the desk, until he was right by Strickland's swivel chair. He reached his hand up to feel the top of the desk. The almanac had to be up there somewhere. There! His fingers brushed it. If he could just . . .

Strickland's chair creaked as he turned. His knee crushed Marty's hand against the desk. Somehow, Marty managed to pull his hand free. Somehow, he also managed not to yell. The vice-principal turned back to the desk, sticking his knees right in Marty's face!

But then Strickland leaned back in his chair to stare out the window one more time. Marty knew right where the book was now. It might be a little riskier with Strickland this much closer, but all Marty needed was one good grab. He leaned forward . . .

And Strickland turned back to the desk. Marty pushed himself back as he heard the vice-principal stick the bottle back in the drawer and then push the drawer shut.

Strickland stood. He looked like he was ready to leave. And, as he walked away, Marty saw the vice-principal's hands were empty. He wasn't taking the sports book with him. Maybe Marty could get hold of the sports almanac at last. The vice-principal took a step away, then looked back, and picked up the book!

Oh, no! Marty didn't want to start this all over again!

Strickland walked to the door—and threw the book into the wastebasket at the corner of the desk!

Marty started breathing again. At last! He waited for Strickland to leave the office, then scrambled from his hiding place to grab the book from the trash. Here it was, with its red and silver dust jacket: *Grey's Sports Almanac*.

The book fell open as Marty grabbed it. His mouth fell open, too, when he saw the pages, full of photos of scantily clad women! Marty pulled off the dust cover. Underneath was *Ooh-La-La*, one of Biff's girlie magazines! "Shit!" Marty yelled. He couldn't believe this!

He pulled his walkie-talkie out of his pocket.

"Doc!" he said as he pressed the talk button. "Trouble. I blew it." He quickly described what had happened to him.

"Where's the book?" Doc's voice answered him.

Marty hadn't even thought about that. "Biff must still have it on him!"

"Where's Biff?" Doc asked.

"I don't know!" Marty exclaimed, his voice close to despair.

He looked out the window of Strickland's office. He could see out to the parking lot. There was George McFly, hiking up his pants, getting ready to go over to the Packard. If only, Marty thought, everything they had to do had stayed as simple as that!

"Don't you have any idea where he is?" Doc demanded.

"No, Doc," Marty replied grimly. "He could be anywhere by now. For all I know he could have hopped a Greyhound and left town!"

"Great Scott!" Doc exclaimed. "This is serious shit!"

"Tell me about it!" Marty answered, ready to descend into misery.

"Think, Marty, think!" Doc insisted. "Where would Biff have gone?"

Marty shook his head. "Doc, if I knew that, I'd go after him."

But Doc just wouldn't let it go. "Marty, the entire future depends on your finding Biff and getting that book back!"

"I know, Doc. I just don't know where to—"

Marty stopped. Somebody was yelling outside. It was Lorraine.

"Stop it, Biff!" she screamed. "You'll break his arm!"

Lorraine? George? Biff?

Biff was still out there! Even though Biff had gotten the sports almanac, and Marty had come back here to try to get it back, nothing had really changed about that night at the "Enchantment Under the Sea" dance. Biff and George were still going to have their confrontation! And Marty could still get the book!

"Of course!" Marty shouted into the walkie-talkie. "I got one more chance! I'll call you back!"

"Roger, ten-four," Doc replied with relief. "Message acknowledged. Standing by."

Marty ran to the office door, unlocked the dead bolt, and took off. He'd have to time this just right, but it could work. It had to!

• • •

It was happening all over again. Except, Marty reminded himself, it was really happening for the first time. It was him that was repeating.

He had stopped at the edge of the parking lot, half hidden by the other cars. There, in front of him, were the events that would lead to his mother and father marrying and having a family—Marty included!

Biff and George were facing off.

"Leave him alone!" Lorraine cried. She tried to stop Biff, but the burly teenager knocked her down and out of the way. Biff laughed.

And George got pissed! His fingers closed into a fist, his teeth clenched, and he let Biff have it, right in the kisser!

Biff crumpled. He was out cold!

"Way to go, George!" Marty whispered to himself. But there was the other Marty, running onto the scene! The later version ducked behind the car.

He knew what happened next, anyway. He should; he'd been there.

"Talk about déjà vu . . ." Marty whispered.

Now, George and Lorraine would walk off together, arm-in-arm, the beginning of a beautiful romance. A crowd would gather around the unconscious Biff. And Marty, the other, earlier Marty, would check that photo—the one where he and his brother and sister were all disappearing, because he had changed the past.

Then the earlier Marty would run off again, too. And that was the here-and-now Marty's chance!

Marty peeked up over the car. Yep, there was his earlier self, leaving right on schedule.

Now it was time for the new Marty to take over.

He ran down to the crowd and pushed his way toward Biff.

"Let me through," Marty called. "I know CPR!"

A scrawny kid looked up at him with a frown.

"CPR?" he asked. "What's CPR?"

What was the scrawny kid's problem? Everybody knew what CPR was, didn't they? Oh, that's right, Marty realized. They probably didn't, back in 1955.

Marty bent down over Biff.

"Everybody, move back," he shouted to the crowd. "Give him some air."

The crowd obliged, stepping back enough to give Marty some breathing room.

Biff groaned. He was coming to. He blinked as his eyes focused on Marty.

"Hey!" Biff shouted angrily. "What the—*you!*"

There was only one thing to do. Marty slugged him all over again—smack in the jaw. Biff obligingly passed out. Marty just hoped not too many people in the crowd noticed that little maneuver.

He quickly rolled the other teenager over and lifted up his jacket. There was the sports almanac, still stuck into the waistband of Biff's pants. Marty pulled it free, rapidly flipping through the pages full of row after row of sports scores—just to make sure. This was the real thing at last.

Marty sighed. It was good to have *that* over with. He stood up and turned to the crowd.

"It's okay, everybody," he said in a loud, calm, clear voice. "He's gonna be fine.

The scrawny kid stared at Marty in suspicion.

"Hey," he whined, "did you just take his wallet?"

Marty shook his head and pushed his way through the crowd. It was time to get out of here before anything else happened. He walked quickly back toward the school.

"He just took this guy's wallet!" the scrawny guy yelled to the crowd. But nobody seemed to be listening. At least Marty hoped they weren't.

He stepped back into the shadows and pulled out his walkie-talkie.

"Yo, Doc!" he called, holding up the sports almanac as if Doc Brown might be able to see it. "Success! I've got it!"

Doc replied, "Thank goodness! I'll be on my way as soon as I reload Mr. Fusion. I'll pick you up on the roof of the gym!"

"The roof of the gym!" Marty replied. "Ten-four!"

He shoved the walkie-talkie in one jacket pocket, the almanac in another. Now, to get to the top of the gym, and get this whole thing over with for good. Marty had to admit it; he'd be glad when all this was history.

He heard the song "Earth Angel" coming from the gym as he climbed the stairs. He remembered the dance band—the Starlighters. It had been fun to play with them that time—the last time he was here.

Marty realized there were three pairs of legs, male legs, coming down the stairs toward him.

He looked up, and saw Match, 3-D, and Skinhead coming his way.

Marty turned around and went the other way.

"Hey!" Skinhead yelled as Marty went from a walk to a run. "That was him! In disguise! He got out!"

"The Calvin Klein creep?" 3-D added. "How'd he change his clothes?"

But Match had a simple solution to all of this.

"Let's get him!"

Marty's heart sank as he heard three pairs of shoes clumping heavily down the stairs after him.

Wouldn't this be over—ever?

•Chapter
Nineteen•

Marty ran into the gym again. He headed immediately for the shadows behind the refreshment table. The fewer people who saw him, the better!

He looked over at the stage and saw his other self, introducing "Johnny B. Goode." Wow! He'd never seen himself perform before. He didn't look bad, in the coat and tie and all, up there on stage. Now, if Marty could just get rid of Biff's gang somehow, he could actually stand here for a minute and enjoy his act!

Biff's boys came through the same door Marty had used. Marty ducked down behind the refreshment table. It was pretty dark, here in the corner. Maybe he could get rid of them, after all.

"Look!" 3-D said to the others. "How'd he get on stage?"

"Yeah!" Match added. "And he changed clothes again!"

"I don't know," Skinhead growled back. "But when he gets down, we'll be waitin' for him! C'mon!"

Oh, no! Marty had lost them all right, but only because he'd led them right to the earlier version of Marty! He moved down to the end of the refreshment table, only to see the three gang members now standing off in the right-hand wings backstage, waiting until they could get their hands on the other Marty!

What could Marty—either of the Martys—do?

The one with the walkie-talkie decided he'd better call Doc.

Doc Brown wandered around the future home of Lyon Estates, looking for dead leaves, old beer cans, and any other trash he might be able to use in his Mr. Fusion drive.

The walkie-talkie crackled to life in his pocket. Doc pulled it out as Marty started to speak.

"Doc! Biff's guys chased me into the gym and now they're laying for me!"

Marty seemed to be getting a little upset by all this. But that was one of the reasons Doc was here, after all, as a calming influence.

"Then go out another door," he suggested reasonably.

"No," Marty explained frantically, "they're laying for the *other* me: the one that's on stage, playing 'Johnny B. Goode'!"

"Great Scott!" Doc replied. This *was* serious. Even the ramifications of something like this had ramifications!

"If they succeed," he explained to Marty, "you'll miss the lightning bolt at the clock tower, you won't get back to the future—and we'll have a major paradox."

"A paradox?" Marty asked. "You mean one of those things that could destroy the universe?"

Doc couldn't have said it better himself.

"Precisely!"

"This is heavy!" Marty agreed.

Doc thought for a second. They had been so close to success—and now this! There had to be some way out of this, didn't there?

"Marty," he said back into the walkie-talkie. "You have to stop those guys at all costs—but without being seen by your other self, or your parents!"

There—that pretty much summed up exactly what Marty had to do, or else.

So why didn't Doc feel any better about this?

"Ten-four," Marty replied, putting away the walkie-talkie. So all he had to do was stop these guys without letting the other Marty, or just about anybody else, see him, right? Hey, piece of cake—if only he could figure out how.

One thing was certain—he wasn't going to get anything done standing behind the refreshment table. He should probably get up on that stage himself—maybe in the wings opposite where the gang was standing. He walked behind the refreshment table one more time, keeping to the edges of the gym, circumnavigating the dance. No one stopped him—no one even noticed him much—and both the guitar-playing Marty and Biff's boys were busy doing their own things. It was easy to make it to the steps leading up to the stage—but now what?

But Marty knew what happened next, since, after all, he'd done it before himself. It was time for the guitar-playing Marty to go into his solo, and once he did that, he'd be oblivious to the world! Yep! Here came those first fractured chords!

Marty shot up the stairs and into the wings, stage left.

So far, so good, Marty thought. But, not to repeat himself—now what?

He didn't have any ideas until he looked overhead.

There were some awfully heavy sandbags over this stage.

Marty found a catwalk ladder and started to climb.

Mr. Fusion was filled at last. Doc climbed into the DeLorean and set the destination display for good old 1985. Better to do it now, he figured. Heaven knew how fast he would have to get Marty out of whatever he'd gotten himself into at the high school.

He started the DeLorean up and lifted it smoothly

from the ground. He cleared the billboard in a matter of seconds.

But somebody was coming down the road, on the other side! It was a pickup truck. The truck screeched to a halt as soon as the driver spotted the flying car.

Doc realized that truck looked awfully familiar, what with the repainted sign on the door and all, even before old man Peabody jumped out brandishing his shotgun.

Doc decided it was time to get out of here. He started to perform the sort of thing they always called "evasive maneuvers" as Peabody aimed and fired.

Doc threw the DeLorean into a mini-nosedive so it swooped almost to the ground, and then began climbing again, right into the real-estate pennants hanging from the Lyons Estates sign! He heard cloth rip as the pennants got caught on the underside of the DeLorean. Oh, well, Doc thought, it wasn't the end of the world if he dragged a few cloth flags along with him. Just so long as he got out of here as quickly as possible! He blasted toward town, streaming a row of multicolored pennants behind him.

"Come back here, you space varmint!" old man Peabody called after him.

But by then the DeLorean—even carefully flown at under eighty-eight miles per hour—was gone.

• • •

Biff groaned. He was coming around. Lester was glad he waited. When Biff woke up, Lester would tell him all about that other guy and what he did. Yeah, Lester would!

Biff opened his eyes and rubbed his jaw. He sat up, and blinked like he was having trouble remembering where he was. He reached back to hike up his pants, then frowned and felt along his back.

"What the hell?" Biff muttered. He looked down at the lawn, as if he was missing something.

Lester knew it. He just knew it!

"He stole your wallet, didn't he?" Lester asked, trying not to spit despite his excitement.

"Huh?" Biff replied.

"That kid took something off you while you were lying there!" Lester exclaimed, almost clapping his hands that he might actually be right for a change. "I knew it was your wallet!"

Biff scowled at Lester.

"What kid?" Biff demanded. "Who?"

"A little guy in a leather jacket," Lester replied. "I don't know his name." He backed up a little, despite himself. Biff wouldn't hurt him, would he? Lester was *helping* him!

"Where did he go?" Biff asked darkly.

Oh, good. Biff wasn't going to beat up Lester. He was going to beat up the other guy. He pointed at the back door of the gym. "That way."

Biff pushed Lester out of the way and lumbered toward the gym. Lester grinned. He had done a good thing. Now maybe Biff and his boys wouldn't beat him up again for two weeks, maybe three!

Biff growled as he flung the fire door aside. Boy, Lester thought, he wouldn't want Biff beating him up when he was angry.

That could get really serious.

This plan had made a lot more sense when he had been on the ground.

Marty looked at the catwalk in front of him. Actually, you couldn't even call it a catwalk. It was really only a pair of long bars that the lights hung from—two bars that stretched high across the stage. And those bars were covered with a thick layer of dust. They looked like they hadn't been touched in years!

But there wasn't time for another plan. The other Marty was halfway through his guitar solo! He had to get over to the other side of the stage, before his other self got demolished by Biff's gang!

The bars swung sickeningly back and forth as Marty grabbed them. No time for another plan, he told himself again, and quickly hoisted himself onto the bars so that he had a hand and foot on each of them. Now, he reasoned, all he had to do was crawl across.

The right bar swung away from him. Marty felt his right foot slip free and fall through space, straight toward his guitar-playing double! He twisted wildly back toward his left, and, somehow, managed to regain his balance without losing his grip.

He crawled across the rest of the twin bars slowly, carefully, reaching out one hand, then one foot, then the other hand and foot, until he finally made it to the other side of the stage, where he could get a firm grip on an iron support pole. But he'd made it to the sandbags, too—fifteen or twenty of them, all tied together in one, big bundle. And there, almost directly underneath him, were the three hoods.

Marty quickly untied all but one slipknot on the bunch of sandbags. 3-D and the others were standing down there, watching as his other self played those last wild chords. And those chords were wild. My, Marty thought, he had gotten a little carried away there toward the end, hadn't he?

He pulled the ropes.

The sandbags fell.

They wiped out all three of the hoods.

Marty grabbed one of the free ropes and swung down to the very back of the backstage. There was a set of stairs over here that led to the same alcove he had come in through!

Marty pulled out his walkie-talkie as he took the steps, two at a time.

"Success, Doc! Everything's cool!"

"Good!" Doc's voice replied after the usual burst of static. "I'll be landing at the school roof in about one minute."

Marty pushed the fire door open. He had to get back around the building to the outside fire stairs and the top of the gym.

"I'll be there, Doc!" He shut off the walkie-talkie and thrust it back in his pocket.

He glanced back in the window of the fire door. There, in the alcove he had just left, was Lorraine, talking to the other Marty!

"I had a feeling about you two," the other Marty was saying.

"I have a feeling, too," Lorraine replied with the sweetest smile.

Marty ducked down as he hurried past the window, glad that everything had worked out, again. Just like they learned in English class: All's well that ends well.

"Hey," a voice yelled behind him, "butthead!"

Marty spun around. Biff stood next to the fire door, rubbing at a raw spot where he'd cut his lip. Biff grinned and waved for Marty to come closer.

"C'mon, let's have it out!" he demanded. "You and me!"

Oh, no, Marty thought. Not when he was so close to being out of here. He grinned back at Biff.

"No, thanks," he replied brightly as he turned to leave.

Biff took a step toward him. "What's the matter?" he called after the retreating Marty. "Chicken?"

Marty stopped dead.

"Too chicken to take me on," Biff jeered, "one-on-one?"

Marty turned around, his hands clenched into fists. There was only one thing he couldn't stand.

"Nobody calls me chicken," he replied.

•Chapter Twenty•

Marty knew this was stupid, but he couldn't help himself. His mother always told him to count to ten—but when it came to this, he was way beyond counting! Maybe he always felt he needed to do this because he was so short. Or maybe he needed to do this just because Biff was such an asshole.

Whatever it was—he didn't let anybody call him chicken!

Biff and Marty stared at each other for a long moment. Marty felt as if all his senses had been heightened. He could feel his heart beating in his chest, and could hear the crickets on the high school lawn, the cars passing on the distant street, and even the voice of the other Marty, who spoke to George and Lorraine on the other side of the fire door.

"If you guys ever have kids," the other Marty was

saying, "and one of them—when he's eight years old—accidentally sets fire to the living room rug, go easy on him."

"C'mon," Biff said, breaking the spell. "Take a poke at me, chicken."

All right. If that's the way Biff wanted it.

As Marty took a step forward, the fire door swung open, smack into his face.

Marty fell to the ground, stunned. He had been knocked down by the earlier version of himself who was running off to rendezvous with the other Doc for the clock tower lightning bolt. Marty blinked and realized that the almanac had fallen out of his pocket and was laying on the ground next to him.

Biff realized it, too.

"What the hell?" Biff demanded, bending over Marty to pick up the almanac. "Steal my stuff will ya' punk?" He grabbed the sports almanac from the ground.

Marty groaned in pain as Biff kicked him in the gut, one, two, three times.

"And this is for my car!" Biff added, kicking him once more, even harder than before. The pain was like fire.

"Butthead!" Biff called over his shoulder as he walked to his car.

Marty moaned as he clutched his stomach. No matter how much it hurt, he had to get up and follow Biff.

He managed to get to his knees. He saw Biff throw

the sports book into the backseat, then get in the car and drive away.

There was no way Marty could chase Biff. Marty was having enough trouble just getting on his feet. He swayed unsteadily as he finally forced both his sneakers beneath him and slowly stood. He took a couple of careful breaths. Everything seemed to be all right. He was bruised, but nothing was broken.

He had to meet Doc! His arms hugging his sore sides, Marty headed for the metal stairs that led to the roof of the gym.

Marty was a little late. Oh, well, it gave Doc a chance to untangle all these pennants from the drive mechanism of the DeLorean. But, once he had the whole rope's length of them all rolled up, what could he do with the roll?

He tossed the ball of pennants in the back of the DeLorean. One of these days, he would have to clean up back there.

He turned as he heard a groan behind him.

Great Scott! It was Marty. But his face was smudged, his clothing torn. He looked like he'd been run over by a truck!

Marty tried to smile at Doc as he struggled up the last few steps of the metal ladder.

Doc rushed over to help him onto the roof.

"Marty!" Doc asked as he helped Marty from the ladder. "What happened?"

Marty shook his head.

"I blew it, Doc! Biff nailed me and got the book back. He drove off with it in his car."

Doc looked back down over the roof. He could see no sign of Biff or his old Ford convertible.

"Which way did he go?" he asked Marty.

Marty thought for a minute as he managed to stand on his own.

"East."

Doc told Marty to get in the DeLorean. They had a job to do.

Marty felt better, once he got his breath back. He'd be sore for a couple of days, but otherwise, he felt all right. Doc was flying the DeLorean east, following the main highway out of town. Now all Marty had to do was concentrate on sweeping the area below them with his binoculars until he found Biff.

He saw a single car, really tearing down the highway. He looked through the binoculars. Yeah! It was Biff, all right! Marty could even see the sports almanac on the backseat!

He pointed down at the car beneath the flying DeLorean. "That's him, Doc! We can just land right on top of him and cripple his car!"

But Doc frowned and shook his head.

"No, Marty, we can't risk damaging the DeLorean. We don't want to be stuck here in 1955."

Marty looked down at Biff's car, then back at Doc. "Then what do we do?" he asked.

Doc grinned at Marty. Marty knew that smile. Doc had a plan.

Boy, Marty had to admit it, when Doc came up with a plan, it was a *plan*.

It also helped that Doc never cleaned out the rear section of the DeLorean. It seemed there was still a certain pink hoverboard back there—the one a little girl had given to Marty in the future!

Doc turned off his headlights and brought the DeLorean down so that it almost brushed the ground, then eased it forward so that it was almost touching the Ford's rear bumper.

The rest was up to Marty.

He opened the gull-wing door and tucked his left foot snugly into the strap at the rear of the hoverboard. Then he pushed the hoverboard out of the car, and, while still keeping one hand on the DeLorean, was soon hoverboarding over nothing but air!

Now, all Marty had to do was move forward along the DeLorean, and grab some part of Biff's car. He pushed the hoverboard forward, skating across the space between the cars.

There! Marty grinned as he grabbed hold of Biff's rear bumper. He waved at Doc with his free hand. Doc waved in return, then lifted the DeLorean back up into the sky.

Biff was blasting the radio and had his foot down on the gas. But he wasn't even glancing in his rear-view mirror. And the book was in the backseat, only a few feet away.

Marty moved into position. But just as he prepared to grab the almanac, the sports news had come on the radio—and Biff reached around to grab the book. As Biff turned, Marty ducked, squatting on the hoverboard to hide himself outside the car.

"In college football today," the sports announcer droned, "UCLA defeated Washington, nineteen to seventeen; Stanford over Oregon, twenty-four to ten . . ."

"Son of a bitch!" Biff muttered. Marty's heart sank. Biff had found that the scores were really in there. It would be twice as hard to get the book now.

But he still had to try. Marty waited a minute, then raised himself slowly, only to see Biff drop the book on the front passenger seat.

Double damn! Marty thought. The book had been so close! But he told himself to calm down. Biff was just making this a little more challenging.

Marty ducked down low again so his head was below window level, and pulled himself forward using the door handles. If Biff was going to leave the book in the front seat, Marty would simply have to go up to the front seat.

Marty reached the front door. He grabbed the handle, and pushed the button. The door swung open.

Marty reached his arm inside the car, just above seat level. His fingers closed around the almanac.

Then Biff looked over at the passenger seat.

"Hey!" Biff yelled.

He saw Marty's hand on the sports book. Biff grabbed the book, too, and looked up at Marty, standing inside the open door.

"You again!" Biff screamed.

Marty tried to pull the book toward him, but Biff had too strong a grip. Maybe, Marty thought, he'd have to get all the way into the car.

But Biff had other ideas. He picked his right foot off the accelerator, and stuck his left foot there instead. He kicked his right foot out, against the door, forcing it open with Marty still on it.

Marty lost his grip on the book. But Biff had lost his hold, too.

The overmuscled teen took his foot off the gas as the sports almanac went flying. It landed on the hood, and the wind whipped it onto the windshield.

Marty had to get that book, now.

He started to pull himself up past the door, up toward the windshield.

To his surprise, Biff didn't try to stop him. Instead, the burly teenager grinned, and floored the gas pedal.

Doc had put the DeLorean on autopilot so he could watch everything below on his own set of mini-binoculars—except when the occasional cloud got in the way. It was taking far too long! If only there was some other way he could help Marty! But he couldn't get any closer. He'd risked showing the DeLorean far too much already.

He saw Marty reach the front of the car and ac‑
tually get his hand on the book. But then Biff had
it, too, and, after a brief tug-of-war, it ended up on
the windshield! Marty started pulling himself to‑
ward the book again . . .

There was another one of those pesky clouds.

Oh, no! There was a hill up ahead—Deacon's Hill,
as Doc recalled—which meant they were coming up
to the Deacon's Hill Tunnel! And Marty was so busy
trying to get that book, he wasn't paying any atten‑
tion to where Biff's car was going!

Biff swerved the car to the right. He was going to
wipe Marty off the side of his car like an insect.

Doc pulled out his walkie-talkie.

"Marty!" he yelled. "Look out!"

But the DeLorean was already flying over the hill,
and Doc lost sight of Biff's car below.

If only he had been in time!

• Chapter
Twenty-One •

Marty had almost bought it.

He had turned the second he heard Doc's warning, and seen the tunnel coming up fast!

He let go of the car, more from panic than from any plan. The hoverboard fell back away from the speeding Ford as Marty grabbed the rear bumper, barely swinging himself away from the wall, as Biff threw the car to the right. Sparks flew as Biff scraped the side of the car against the rough brick of the tunnel.

But Marty was still here, hanging onto the back of Biff's car. And he was still going to get that sports almanac.

He started to move the hoverboard forward again, this time on the driver's side.

All he had to do was keep low as he pulled himself past Biff.

Marty glanced up and saw Tannen grinning at him in the side-view mirror. He couldn't duck fast enough. Biff socked him in the ear, hard.

His head ringing, Marty almost lost his grip. Somehow he managed to hold onto the windshield. Biff swung at him again, but this time Marty was ready. He dodged the blow as Biff had to throw his hands back on the wheel to straighten out the car.

Biff jerked the wheel left. He was going to try to crush Marty against the other wall.

Marty had to get out of here.

There was the sound of an air horn, and Marty saw two truck headlights headed straight for them! Biff swung the car back into the right lane, and the truck missed Marty by inches. It was a dump truck of some sort. Marty watched it travel away from them through the tunnel for a second until he felt Biff jerk the car back into the left lane. They were awfully close to the other wall. Marty had to do something!

But then he remembered how, when he had been in the future, the hoverboard had been able to skate over more than just the ground. In fact, it could go over anything but water! Maybe, he thought, he should stop trying to avoid the wall and lean the hoverboard into it, instead.

Yes! It really worked. Still holding the side of the windshield, he pushed the hoverboard away from the car and skated up the side of the tunnel! And—

this was even better than he thought!—going up the tunnel wall brought him above the hood of the car, that much closer to the sports almanac.

He grabbed the book.

Biff reached over the windshield in a wild grab for Marty.

"You son of a bitch!" he yelled.

But Marty simply let go of the car. The Ford shot ahead, and Marty, no longer sharing in the car's acceleration, fell behind. He shoved the almanac in his inside jacket pocket as his hoverboard glided to a halt. He zipped the jacket up, and started kickpushing the hoverboard with his free foot toward the end of the tunnel where they had come in.

He heard a squeal of tires behind him. Marty glanced back as he tried to kick the hoverboard forward with greater speed. Biff had stopped, and was turning his car around in the tunnel.

Without a car to tow him along, Marty could only go as fast on this hoverboard as he could kick it, just like the skateboards Marty was used to. But he had to get out of this tunnel before Biff caught up to him.

He just hoped he could kick this sucker fast enough!

So where was Marty?

Doc had kept the DeLorean hovering over the exit to the tunnel for the last minute, expecting Biff's car to show up at any second. But there was no sign of Biff, and no sign of Marty—no sign of anything, really, except a big old truck carrying fertilizer that had gone into the tunnel beneath him.

Gone into the tunnel?

Oh no, Doc Brown thought, Marty didn't have to come out this way at all.

He raised the DeLorean quickly. He only hoped he wasn't too late to rectify his error.

Oh, shit.

Marty saw the mouth of the tunnel in front of him. But he could hear Biff behind him, coming on fast. And Marty couldn't push the hoverboard any harder. His leg felt like it was going to fall off, and his ribs had started aching all over again.

But he couldn't stop now. He was so close to the mouth of the tunnel, so close to getting away.

He didn't want to look back again. He expected to get run over by two tons of Ford convertible at any second.

Marty kicked even harder.

Pout it on, McFly! Pour it on!

He swore he could hear Biff laughing, over the sound of the revving engine.

Oh, God!

The tunnel mouth was just in front of him, but Marty had no energy left. Even his adrenalin was all used up!

Biff's car roared behind him. Marty had never heard a car sound so loud. Kick! He had to kick!

A rope tied with multicolored pennants dropped

down in front of him. It looked like the rope from a used-car lot—or the Lyon Estates sign!

Marty grabbed it and felt himself being lifted aloft, the hoverboard still strapped to his foot.

Marty looked up.

Doc waved down at him from the open door of the DeLorean.

Marty looked down and saw Biff's astonished face as his old Ford sped through the space where Marty had been only a second ago. By the time Biff turned his eyes back to the road and saw that slow-moving fertilizer truck just ahead, it was much too late for him to put on the brakes or get out of the way.

"Shit!" Biff screamed as the Ford smashed into the truck.

Then tons of manure fell down to silence him.

•Chapter
Twenty-Two•

The wind was picking up.

Marty hung onto the pennant rope as Doc flew the DeLorean a safe distance away from Biff. Even if the burly teenager was currently covered by manure, neither one of them wanted to take any chances. But the increasing gusts of wind were blowing the rope back and forth in ever bigger and more dangerous arcs. There was no way Marty could call Doc on the walkie-talkie, either; he had to use all his strength just to hang on.

But Doc must have seen Marty's problem, too, about the time the Lyons Estate billboard came back into sight. He brought the DeLorean down low enough for Marty to jump from the rope—and Marty decided he'd better do just that. The hoverboard helped to break his fall, anyway. Marty put his free foot on the ground and slipped his other foot out of the hoverboard strap. He looked up at the DeLorean as a bolt of lightning streaked across the sky.

That's right! In all the excitement, Marty had almost forgotten: This was the night of the big lightning storm—the same night Doc had last sent him back to the future!

The wind was nearing gale force. Marty could see the DeLorean rock overhead, buffeted by the turbulence.

He pulled out his walkie-talkie. "Yo, Doc! Is everything all right—over?"

He saw Doc slam the car door firmly shut overhead, with the pennant cord still hanging down. There was a burst of static on the radio.

"Ten-four, Marty," Doc answered on the walkie-talkie. "But it's pretty miserable flying weather— much too turbulent to make a landing from this direction. I'll have to circle around and make a long approach from the south."

There was another burst of static as lightning streaked the sky.

"Have you got the book?" Doc asked.

Marty could feel the sports almanac inside his jacket.

"Check, Doc!" he called back.

Another burst of static, then Doc's response: "Burn it!"

Burn it? Wasn't Doc overreacting a little? Why burn a perfectly good key to the future? But then Marty realized that Doc was right; it was because this book *was* a perfectly good key to the future that it had to be burned! As long as this book existed where it shouldn't be, there was always a chance that Biff, or somebody even worse, could get hold of it and change the future back into something like that terrible version of 1985 they had so recently escaped.

So he had to burn it, but in this wind? Marty decided he'd better go over and use the billboard as protection against the storm. He could feel a matchbook in his pocket. He pulled it out and looked at it. It was the same black and white book he'd picked up when he was back in 1985—the bad 1985.

He looked at the matchbook in his hand, the bold black letters on white:

BIFF'S PLEASURE PARADISE

So he was going to burn up the sports almanac with a matchbook advertising the business empire that very same almanac had made possible? Marty liked that. There was a certain justice there.

He struck a match and held the flame under one corner of the sports almanac. The paper caught right away and, a moment later, the book was in flames. Marty let the burning book drop as he glanced at the matchbook in his other hand.

The lettering on the matchbook had changed. It now read:

BIFF'S AUTO DETAILING

Biff's Auto Detailing? But that was what Biff had done in 1985—that is, the real 1985, the 1985 Marty had come from when this whole thing started!

Did that mean other things had changed, too?

Marty reached into his back pants pocket and pulled out the folded piece of newspaper he had ripped out of that bound library volume.

No. The smile left Marty's face. Maybe it wasn't as simple as that. There was the headline, still.

GEORGE MCFLY MURDERED

But, as Marty stared at the page, the headline changed.

GEORGE MCFLY HONORED

The picture below changed, too. It now showed his father accepting the book award!

They'd done it. They'd changed the future! 1985 had gone back to the way it should be!

"The newspaper changed, Doc!" Marty yelled into the walkie-talkie. "My father's alive! Everything's back to normal!"

Could it be?

Doc Brown ignored the wind rocking the De-Lorean long enough to pull out the newspaper article he'd saved from that awful 1985. There it was, his none-too-desirable future:

But, wait a minute! The last word wasn't "committed" anymore! No, his article had changed, too! It now read:

EMMETT BROWN COMMENDED

And beneath that, in a subheading:
"Local Inventor Receives College Grant."
Really? A college grant, hmm? Oh, that's right! Doc remembered now. There he was, with those two fellows handing him that handsome placard as recognition for the years he had spent as the professor of physics at the local university.

Doc sighed with relief. Everything had been corrected. The future was now restored to the way it was supposed to be, and the proof was right there in the newspaper. Had he not been sitting in the car, Doc would have jumped for joy! Mission accomplished! All that remained was a simple matter of logistics. Doc would pick up Marty and they would go back to the future . . . actually their own present, October 26, 1985. And this time it would be the same 1985 they had left from on the morning of October 26, 1985.

Doc sighed again. Finally, the adventure was over!

•Epilogue•

A bolt of lightning streaked through the sky, much too close to the DeLorean. It hit a tree across the road from the billboard. A large branch crashed to the ground.

Marty pressed the "talk" button on his walkie-talkie.

"Doc! You okay?"

Doc's voice replied through the ever-increasing static: "That was a close one, Marty!" Doc laughed ruefully. "I almost bought the farm!"

The DeLorean started to move overhead, as Doc turned the flying car around to begin his approach. Marty knew just what Doc was thinking—they had to get out of here before something serious happened!

The DeLorean started toward Marty, swooping down out of the sky.

Then a bolt of lightning, even bigger than the last one, streaked out of the sky to hit the DeLorean.

There was a noise even louder than a sonic boom!

Marty threw his hands in front of his face, temporarily blinded by the light.

But when he uncovered his eyes and looked up again, the sky was empty. Oh, there were the heavy clouds and the lightning, but the DeLorean flying toward him only a second ago was gone!

The pennant cord fluttered to the ground in front of Marty. The upper end of the cord was still burning. A minute ago, it had been hanging out of the DeLorean's door. Was that all that was left of the time machine?

No! Marty thought. That was silly. This was a time machine we were talking about here! A time machine didn't just disappear, did it? It had to be around someplace, didn't it? Even if the car had somehow gotten zapped and pushed into the wrong time, all Doc had to do was reset the destination display and bring the DeLorean back, didn't he?

Well, Marty added to himself, that should make sense. So where was Doc?

He yelled into his walkie-talkie again. "Yo, Doc! Come in Doc!"

There was no response.

Marty tried again. "Hello, Doc, do you read me, over?"

There was nothing on the walkie-talkie but static.

"Doc, answer me, please!"

He was answered instead by another blinding flash of lightning, followed by a great boom of thunder and pouring rain.

This stuff was coming down hard! Marty had to find cover somewhere! He ducked quickly behind the Lyon's Estates billboard. There was just enough of an awning overhead to leave a couple feet dry back here.

Somebody had also left a bicycle behind the billboard. It still had the price tag on the handlebars. That's right! Doc had gotten around town on a bike, hadn't he?

Doc, Marty thought. What had happened to him?

Marty stepped out from behind the billboard.

"Doc!" he yelled one more time, but his voice was lost in the storm.

Through the rain, Marty saw a pair of headlights coming down the road from the direction of town.

Maybe, Marty thought, he'd better get back out of sight; he didn't want any more complications than he already had. He stepped behind the billboard again and leaned the hoverboard against the sign, right next to the bike.

The car stopped on the other side of the billboard. What was going on now? For a wild second, Marty was afraid that Biff had somehow gotten out of the manure! Marty peeked around the edge of the sign. No, the car was some kind of dark sedan. Marty didn't recognize it.

A man wearing a hat and trench coat stepped out of the car.

"Hello?" the guy with the trench coat yelled. "Anyone here?"

Who was this guy? It was hard to tell in the darkness and the rain, but Marty could swear he'd never seen him before. And the trench coat and the hat—did that mean he was from the FBI, or something?

"Marty?" the other guy yelled. "Marty McFly?"

The guy knew his name? Marty stopped an urge to run the other way.

"Marty McFly," the guy called over the storm, "if you're here, please show yourself."

Still, this guy hadn't threatened Marty or pulled out a gun or anything. Maybe, Marty thought, he should find out what was going on here.

He stepped out from behind the billboard.

The guy in the trench coat turned his head toward Marty; he had seen him. The way the newcomer was standing in front of his car headlights, though, it was hard for Marty to get a real good look at the other guy's face.

"Is your name Marty McFly?" Trench coat demanded.

Marty almost said it wasn't. But he'd gone this far. He might as well finish this off and find out what was happening.

"Yeah," he answered slowly.

Trench coat looked Marty up and down.

"Five-foot four, brown hair—uh-huh—" he said,

mostly to himself, and then added in a louder voice, "Marty, I've got something for you."

He reached inside his trench coat. Marty took a step back. Did the guy have a gun, after all?

He pulled out a long, thin envelope.

"A letter," Trench coat announced.

"A letter?" Marty asked, taking a closer look at what the other man held in his hand. It was an old, yellowed envelope, with a red wax seal holding it closed.

The other guy reached back inside his trench coat again and pulled out a small clipboard.

"You'll have to sign for it first—" He paused, reaching again inside his coat to search around in some inner pocket. "If I can find a pen."

Marty couldn't believe this.

"You've got a letter for me?" he asked incredulously. "That's impossible! Who are you, anyway?"

Trench coat stepped behind the billboard to get out of the rain.

"I'm from Western Union," he explained, still searching his pockets, "and actually, a bunch of us in the office were hoping *you* could shed some light on the subject."

He smiled at Marty. Actually, the guy didn't look at all threatening, now that he was out of the headlights' glare. Just an average guy, really, around Marty's father's age.

"You see," the guy from Western Union went on, "this envelope's been in our company's possession for seventy years. It was given to us with explicit instructions that it be delivered to a young man with your description answering to the name of Marty at this exact location and at this exact minute on November 12, 1955."

The guy grinned as he pulled a pen from his pocket at last.

"We had a bet going," he continued, "as to whether this 'Marty' would actually be here." Trench coat sighed. "Looks like I lost."

Marty looked back at the letter in the guy's hand. This was still pretty incredible.

"Did you say *seventy* years?"

"That's right." He handed Marty the clipboard and the pen. "Sign on line six, please."

Marty signed, and the other man handed him the letter.

Marty broke open the seal.

He pulled out the yellowed sheets and carefully unfolded them. It was quite a letter, handwritten, a good four pages long. Marty turned to the last page. There, at the bottom, was the signature:

Your friend in time,
"Doc" Emmett L. Brown

And—if there was any doubt that this really was written by Doc Brown, below that was that ridiculously stylized "E—L—B" that Doc always liked to sign his memos and notes with.

"Doc!" Marty said aloud.

He turned to the beginning of the letter and started to read.

Dear Marty:

If my calculations are correct, you will receive this letter immediately after you saw the DeLorean struck by lightning.

First, let me assure you that I am alive and well. I have been living happily in the year 1885 for these past few months—

Marty stopped reading. "1885?" he said aloud.

The Western Union guy tried to lean over Marty's shoulder to get a look at the letter. Marty turned around so the guy in the trench coat couldn't see. After all, he remembered Doc's rules about time travel. And rule one seemed to be: The fewer people who knew about it, the better!

Marty skimmed the rest of the letter quickly, muttering to himself over the good parts.

"Too many jigowatts . . ."

He turned the page.

"Time circuits shorted . . ."

He reached the end of the letter again.

"1885!" he repeated to himself. Doc was stranded back in the wild west. There had to be something Marty could do—and Marty realized just what it was!

He stuffed Doc's letter in his pocket and headed back for town.

"Hey!" the Western Union guy yelled behind him. "Can't you even tell me what this is all about?"

Marty kept on running.

"No?" the Western Union guy called in the most disappointed voice Marty had ever heard.

Marty didn't even look back.

There was no time to lose!

Marty could see it all before him.

The clock tower read 10:04.

The DeLorean, with its special superconducting electrical pole added for the occasion, raced toward the electrical line.

And lightning struck the clock tower!

At the last possible second, after almost falling from a considerable height, Doc Brown connected the cables.

The hook on the pole above the DeLorean hit the electrical line—and 1.21 jigowatts of electricity flooded into the flux capacitor . . .

And the DeLorean vanished into the future, leaving only twin trails of fire where its wheels had been!

Doc Brown—the 1955 version—went running down the street between the twin trails of fire, yelling at the top of his lungs. "Ya—Haaaaa!"

Marty guessed this was as good a time as any.

He stepped out of the shadow of the courthouse. He tapped Doc on the shoulder.

Doc turned around, the smile on his face changing to a look of abject horror.

"Yaaaaaaah!" Doc shrieked.

"Calm, down, Doc," Marty urged. "It's me, Marty!"

Doc shook his head wildly. "No! It can't be you! I just sent you back to the future!"

Somehow, Marty had to explain all of this to the scientist.

"Right!" Marty replied, trying to be as logical as possible. "You *did* send me back to the future. But I came back—back *from* the future!"

"Great Scott!" Doc replied. He staggered back, clutching his chest. He seemed to be having trouble breathing.

"Doc!" Marty called. What was going on?

Doc's eyes rolled up, and he fainted dead away.

"Doc?" Marty asked, but the scientist was out cold. The shock had been too much for him—one of those paradoxes that Doc Brown himself had told Marty about.

But how could Doc help him, if even the scientist couldn't face the truth about the future? And what if it was worse than Marty thought, and he couldn't revive Doc? Then the scientist could never build the time machine, and Marty would never end up back in 1955 in the first place.

That would be one of those real paradoxes, wouldn't it—the kind that might put an end to the cosmos and all life as we know it?

"Doc?" Marty called, bending over his fallen friend. "Doc?"

But Doc didn't answer.

TO BE CONCLUDED

IN

BACK TO THE FUTURE PART III!